DEVIL'S

MUSE

MICHELLE WINDSOR

This one is for Karla and Grace.
For loving music as much as I do, swaying beside me at concerts,
and helping to bring this story to life.
Love you both.
p.s. Karla, I promise one day I'll write you a zombie book.

Chapter One
Lily

Shoot Tequila
Tigirlily Gold

"I REALLY DON'T WANT to do this, Bri." I stand outside the double doors of a hotel suite, the soul of my sneakered foot scuffing back and forth across the floor as I plead to my best friend.

"Of course you do!" She rolls her eyes, always the dramatic one, then continues. "I mean, how often do you personally get invited to an actual rock and roll party, and by a member of one of the biggest bands in the world? You are coming with me, whether you want to or not!"

"But he invited you, not me." I point at myself. "I wasn't even there when he asked you. How do you know it's okay for me to come?"

Bri chuffs, again with another eye roll. "Lily, it's a fucking party thrown by rock stars. I'm pretty sure they're going to be okay with another hot chick in attendance."

Before I can utter another protest, she knocks on one of

the doors. It opens almost immediately, as if someone was standing there waiting, and *oh shit*, listening to our entire conversation. I'm already mortified, and we haven't even walked into the room yet.

A big man, dressed all in black, analyzes us both with a hard stare. "Who are you here with?"

"Yeah, um, Dean invited me." She tosses a glance my way, remembering to include me in the mix. "Us. He invited us. Said to come to this room." All the confidence she exuded a moment ago, fading away as she rambles on. "You know, the guitar player for Devil's Halo."

"I know who Dean is." The man deadpans. Not exactly the friendliest dude. "What's your name?"

"Briana. Briana Chambers." Like a last name really matters right now.

"Hold on." The door shuts in our faces.

"See?" I shuffle away from the door. "We should go. I told you this was a bad idea."

"Will you stop it! Why are you being such-" Her question cut short when the door opens, Dean now standing beside the man in black.

"There you are, you little fox." Dean flirts with Bri. "I've been waiting for you." He grabs her hand, tugging her to his side, his lips planting a kiss against her cheek. "Now the fun can really begin."

Bri's face glows, her cheeks coloring a faint pink as her entire body leans into his, her arm sliding around his back. He pivots them both into the room, Bri's free hand launching out to grasp onto my arm, dragging me behind her. "This is my friend, Lily."

His eyes peruse over me, his head nodding as the corner

of his mouth tilts up in a coy grin. "Cool. I'm game if you are."

I skid to a stop as it clicks that he thinks I'm there to join them for a threesome. I yank my arm out of Bri's grip, my eyes widening as I mouth, *"no way"* to her.

"It's just going to be me and you, if that's okay handsome?" My heart slows its roll as Bri slithers under his arm, pressing her mostly exposed breasts against his chest.

"More than okay." He purrs, and as if it were even possible, his grin cocks up into one more wicked than a moment ago. "Let's get you ladies a drink."

His arm drapes over Bri's shoulders as he steers us further into the suite, straight toward a bar that's set up in the back of an adjoining room. It's enormous, complete with a marble top and leather stools. It sits in front of a bank of twenty-foot-tall windows that overlook the strip, lights twinkling brightly. Every imaginable liquor is displayed behind the bar, lit up underneath in a cool neon red, compliments of a glass LED shelf.

"What'll be ladies?" Dean flashes another easy smile our way as he nods toward the row of choices.

"Tequila shots all around!" Bri shouts, my brow shooting up to my hairline as I curl my fingers around her wrist and squeeze.

Her gaze meets mine, the look she delivers making it very clear I better just shut up and drink. I glare back at her, silently conveying that she's going to owe me big time, releasing the vice grip I have on her. *The things we do for our best friends.*

"You heard her, Eddie," Dean chuckles. "Line 'em up!"

The bartender, who we now know as Eddie, places three shot glasses on the bar and fills them to the brim. A second later, there's a shaker of salt and three wedges of lime next to them.

Dean grins broadly, then lifts his hand to his mouth, his tongue darting out as he presses it flat against the base of his thumb knuckle, before dragging it lazily up to the bottom of the next knuckle. His eyes remain locked on Bri the entire time, his intention with the single action amplified with a salacious wink as he sprinkles the shaker onto his dampened skin.

He licks the trail of salt left behind, then raises the shot, tossing his head back, swallowing the clear liquid in one gulp. His lips pull back to expose a small grimace before swapping the glass for a wedge of lime, which he promptly squeezes between his teeth. "Fuck yeah!"

His attention swings back to us, frowning when he notices neither of us have taken our shot. "What are you waiting for? Giddy up ladies! Knock those suckers back!"

Bri tilts her head to me with a shrug, a wide smile lifting her cheeks as she snags the shot off the counter, taps it against mine before tipping it to her mouth to gulp it down.

I immediately follow suit, not wanting to catch one moment of shit from her for even a second of hesitation, my eyes watering as the tequila burns a trail of heat from my throat to my stomach. I snatch a lime off the counter and suck hard hoping to quell the fire, but it honestly doesn't help much.

"That's what I'm talking about!" Dean hollers as he slaps his palm onto the bar. "Another round, Eddie."

My eyes pop wide at the prospect of doing back-to-back shots of tequila within the span of five minutes, and I shake my head in protest.

"I'm good." I direct my attention to Eddie. "I'll just have a beer."

"Awe, come on, Lily." Bri protests as I snatch the offered bottle off the bar and start backing up. "Let your hair down a little and have some fun!"

"Yeah, what she said." Dean leans over Bri, propping his chin on her shoulder as he slides his arms around her waist. "The fun's just getting started."

"I'm good." I keep backing up, the space between us growing, my eyes darting to the left and right as I try to determine the best escape route, my progress thwarted as I collide into a solid object. I flinch, freezing in place as warm hands land on the exposed skin above the waist of my skirt, fingers gripping my hips lightly.

"Did someone mention fun?" A deep, raspy voice asks from behind, warm breath against my ear a second later as he whispers. "Careful kitten, you might be running *into* more trouble, than away from it."

I spin around, his hold loosening enough for me to do so, but not letting go, and I find myself staring up into the most beautiful eyes I've ever seen.

They're brown, but not just any brown. They look like the color of whiskey, reminding me of the time I stood on the edge of the Grand Canyon as the sun was setting, the cliffs a staggering display of warm brown hues.

They're framed by dark, full lashes, blinking lazily as he stares back at me. The corners start to crinkle as a smile lifts his cheeks. He chuckles then, the vibration from his chest startling me into awareness.

I attempt to move away from him, my face heating under his intensity, but his grip tightens, holding me as his prisoner.

"I thought we were about to have some fun." He's practically growling, his voice still low as he addresses me.

"What?" I stammer, yanking myself free of his grasp, stumbling a bit as I do. "I-I was just going to find a bathroom."

"You need some help with that?" Mr. Whiskey Eyes continues to torment me with his raspy voice and attention.

"Luc, leave the girl alone and come join us for a shot." Dean intervenes, motioning for him with a wave of his arm.

"But she's so pretty." He peers down at me, an almost feral smile flashing my way before addressing Dean. "Are you sure I can't play with her?"

"She's not a toy, asshole." Dean admonishes with a shake of his head. "Get your ass over here and do a shot with us."

"The bathroom's that way." He points to the left as he saunters by me, his scent, cedar and smoke and spice trailing in his wake as I continue to gawk at his beauty.

"Lily?" Bri's voice snaps me out of the trance I've fallen into. "You good?"

"Yep." I give a little wave as I turn to the left. "I'll find you later. Or text me when you're ready." I don't bother waiting for a reply as I scurry away, my skin still tingling from his touch. *What in all things holy was that? Or better yet, who?*

Miraculously, I find the bathroom without further help and secure myself inside, turning the lock before I slump against the door. Why in the hell did I let Bri talk me into going to this party?

I thought I was being pretty damn nice by agreeing to go to the concert of a band I didn't even know, let alone like, for that matter, but to end up at an after party they're throwing? Complete and utter mistake on my part.

I heave out a breath as I push myself upright, then use the

toilet and wash my hands. I glare back at my reflection in the mirror over the sink, knowing I can't be angry at anyone but myself over the predicament I'm in.

I know from past experiences that if Bri wants something, she's going to get it. And holy Hell, she had wanted Dean Ross, the lead guitar player of Devil's Halo, for as long as I could remember.

Not going to lie, the guy was pretty damn nice to look at, but hooking up with someone from a famous rock band-*no thank you*. God knows what kind of medication she's going to need after tonight. Hard pass.

A knock on the door startles me back to reality. "One second," I call out, then unlock the door and stride back out into the unknown. I nod at a guy waiting in the hall. "All yours."

I wander in the opposite direction of the bathroom, wondering what I'll find. I'm not entirely surprised to find a couple dry humping on a couch when I pass a living room area, which I promptly keep walking by.

I continue until I encounter another room, this one furnished with a huge glass table with at least a dozen seats around it. There are seven people sitting at one end, but only one captures my attention.

I pause in the doorway, frozen by the scene unfolding in front of me. There's a half-naked woman lying across the end of the table, narrow rows of white powder lined up perfectly on the curve of her bare hip.

Believe it or not, that's not what has me riveted. It's the fact that Mr. Whiskey Eyes is bent over her ass with a rolled bill in one hand, his other on her waist as he leans over to snort not one, but three rows of the coke. He straightens, throwing his head back in the process, the motion ceasing when his eyes lock onto mine.

One side of his mouth crooks up in a wicked smirk. "See something you like, Kitten?"

My nostrils flare out as I inhale deeply in an attempt to slow down my racing heart. I glare back at him, hating how he is constantly baiting me and calling me a damn kitten. Is that some lame way of referencing I'm just pussy to him?

"I'm all set." I grit out as I twist out of the doorway and barely keep myself from running away.

"Ah, pretty little kitty doesn't want to play." Mocks me from behind as I escape to a staircase I saw earlier. I trot up the stairs, relishing that the hallway at the top is people free. I turn right, roaming further down the hall, knocking on a door, opening it when there's no response. I peek inside to find an empty bedroom.

It's enormous, with a king bed centered on a wall that overlooks the city. The room appears to be unoccupied so I slip inside and shut the door gently, exhaling a sigh of relief. I'll just hang out here until Bri texts me. Hopefully that will be sooner than later.

Chapter Two
Luc

Rockstar
Nickelback

"I'M OUT." I toss my cards on the table and shove my chair back as I stand up. It's only a little after two in the morning, but I'm shattered and ready for bed.

"Oh, come on you fucking pussy, play a few more hands."

My brother, always a goddamn delight to deal with after he's had half a bottle of tequila. "Piss off, Mikey. I said I'm out."

"Why you always gotta be such a little bitch? Do a few more lines if you're tired." He continues to pester me as I stride toward the doorway.

"There's a whole casino downstairs. Why don't you just go down there if you still want to play?"

"And have every single woman crawling all over me the minute they realize who I am?" He sneers back at me. "Not fucking interested."

"Perils of being a Rockstar, I guess," shrugging. "Night, asshole." I toss over my shoulder as I stay my course, heading for the stairs, taking them two at a time when I reach them. We've been on tour for three months, with another one to go, and I'm so over this shit.

A different city every three nights, which means a party for every one of those. My liver is fucking shot. I don't even want to think about what the drugs are doing to my brain. We've got our last show in this city tomorrow, and I just want, no, *need*, a good night's rest.

Chad Kroeger knew what the hell he was talking about when he said life hadn't turned out quite the way he wanted it to. Sure, I love being up on stage. Love performing and the rush I get. The perks of being famous are out of this world. But they come at a price. Peace seemingly one of them. I haven't felt it in a really long time.

I blow out a heavy sigh as I reach my room, grateful I have somewhere quiet to escape to. I turn the knob and push the door open, halting when I realize someone's lying on top of the bed.

I glance down the hall and count doors, confirming I am in fact in the correct room. Fuck me. The last thing I want to deal with right now is a crazy fan.

I take a few more steps into the room, ready to toss whomever this is out on their ass, but stop in my tracks again. A strip of moonlight illuminates her face, and I realize it's the chick that was hanging out with Dean earlier.

The one with the face of an angel, and whose small waist I had my hands around. What in the hell is she doing in here? In my room? She certainly didn't seem too interested in anything I had to offer earlier. Although, I was being a bit of an asshole.

I step closer and kneel down beside the bed to get a closer look. Her hands are in a prayer pose, tucked under her cheek. Cheeks that have a natural spattering of freckles, not the fake, press-on ones all the chicks have been wearing lately.

Her lips, the bottom one puffier than the top, are parted slightly - warm, steady breaths whispering through them at regular intervals. Her long, blonde hair flows out behind her in waves on the pillow.

She's a petite thing. I angle my head as I take in the rest of her, scanning her from head to toe. She's wearing a short white tank top that exposes most of her toned midriff. A little red skirt sits low on her hips, barely covering her ass. What I think are white panties are peeking out from the bottom of said skirt, and it fucking takes everything in me not to lift the hem to verify.

I chuff out a quiet snort when I reach her feet. They're clad in white bobby socks, with curly lace edging and all, under a pair of red chucks. Fucking adorable.

She looks so serene. I hate to wake her, but I want to go to sleep, and I want it to be in my own damn bed. I grip her shoulder to give it a gentle shake. She doesn't respond, so I try again, this time shaking a bit harder.

Her eyes flutter open, widening when they come into focus, a frown pulling down her mouth. "What are you doing here?"

"I was going to ask you the same thing, Kitten." I arch a brow as I rise to my full height and peer down at her.

She shifts to a sitting position, her fingers clutching at the hem of her skirt as she tries to shove it lower. All she succeeds in doing is exposing more skin below her belly button, and I'm not complaining about that one bit.

"I- I'm waiting." She manages to stutter as she presses herself back against the padded headboard, I think in an attempt to put more distance between us.

"Decided you wanted to play after all?" I smirk as I lean over her, placing a hand on either side of her head, bringing my face level with hers. I am tired, but I'm willing to put off a few hours of sleep if it means seeing her naked.

"What?" Her brow scrunches as she shakes her head almost violently. "No!" Her head jerks back until it slams into the padding. "I'm not waiting for you. I'm waiting for my friend."

"As you lay in my bed?" I trace my tongue over my lips as I stare at hers.

"Stop looking at me like that!" She demands as a scowl decorates her face, her cheeks flushing under my gaze.

"You're the one that seems to be everywhere I am tonight." I remind her as I incline a fraction closer, her scent invading my senses. Light and floral, with an undertone of fear peppered in. My favorite.

"Can you please stop?" Her plea barely above a whisper as her eyes dart back and forth from my eyes to my lips. "You're scaring me."

I lock my gaze with hers, absorbing how icy blue her irises are, momentarily losing myself in them until a second plea brings me back to my senses.

"Please." Her dainty hand presses flat against my chest in an attempt to push some space between us.

I huff, then straighten my frame, releasing the headboard as I do, my voice hardening. "So, not waiting for me?"

"I don't even know who you are." She tosses out, wounding my ego a tad.

"Well, you are in my room, in my bed. Don't you think

you should learn who someone is before you lay in wait for them?"

"Cocky much?" She retorts, sitting up straighter before she continues. "This room was empty. I thought it would be okay to wait here for my friend. I didn't know it was yours."

"Uh-huh." I nod. "If I had a nickel for every time I heard that one."

Her scowl deepens as she shifts onto her knees. "Listen, I don't know why you think I'd be up here waiting for you. I don't even know your name. My friend is hanging out with Dean. I'm waiting for her. That's it. Nothing else."

"So, the fact that I'm the lead singer of one of the biggest rock bands in the world has nothing to do with you being in my bed?"

Her eyes practically roll into the back of her head as she snickers. "You really are full of yourself, aren't you?"

"It's a fact." I shrug, widening my stance. "And you shouldn't play with fire if you don't want to get burned."

She huffs out a breath as she crosses her arms, not realizing what it does to her tits. That's how little she heeds my warning.

"Here's a fact for you, I don't even know who your band was before tonight. I am not a fan." She uses her fingers to create air quotes as she exaggerates the word fan. "I only went to the concert because my best friend begged me. And you don't let your best friend down in their time of need."

"And what she needed was to get laid by Dean?"

"I guess." She squeaks out meekly.

"And what you needed was a place to hide out while she did?" I state her now obvious situation.

"I guess." She repeats, then reiterates in a soft voice. "I really didn't know this was anyone's room."

"I believe you." I concede, shoving my hand into my back pocket to grab my phone. "Let me text Dean and see what's what."

"Thank you." Her body relaxes as she leans her backside against her heels. "I appreciate it. Bri isn't answering any of mine."

I type out a quick message to Dean asking him if Bri is still with him and send it. "Well, let's see if Dean answers mine." I hold the phone up so she can see the message I sent.

"Okay." She replies timidly. "Thanks."

"So let me get this straight," I sit on the edge of the bed. "You don't like rock music, or you don't like *our* music?"

"You mean your band's?" She clarifies, her legs curling under her as she adjusts her position. "Devil's Halo, right?"

I throw my head back and bark out a hard laugh. "Yeah. That would be my band."

"Honestly, I'd never listened to you before your concert tonight." She fiddles with a loose string on the bedding as she continues. "I mean, I guess it was okay." Her eyes dart up to meet mine. "It's just not my type of music."

"And what, pray tell, is? For the love of all things sacred, please don't say EDM."

"Club music?" Her nose scrunches. "Ew. No."

"Tell me." I press her for an answer.

"You're just going to make fun of me, so I really don't know what the point is." She volleys back.

"I want to know. I'm genuinely curious." I tilt my head in apprehension.

Her cheeks flush a light pink, her eyes shifting behind me in an attempt to avoid contact. "Country. I'm a country music fan to the core."

I stare at her, assessing her in a new light. She's totally not the groupie I thought she was, that's for sure. I shrug. "Country isn't so bad. Better than fucking techno."

My phone buzzes on the bed next to me and I read the incoming text out loud, regretting it immediately. "Need at least another hour with this delicious pussy." I cringe. "Sorry, should have read that to myself before I shared."

"It's fine." She slaps a hand over her face. "I-" She pauses then gives a small shake of her head. "It's what I signed up for with Bri."

"Guess that leaves us with a slight problem." I muse out loud as I push myself up off the bed to stand.

"Oh! This is your room. I should leave." She puts two and two together, scooting off the bed to stand on the opposite side of me.

"Unless you want to stay?" I grin wickedly taking one more shot at getting her clothes off.

"You don't give up, do you?" Sarcastic laughter following.

"Can't blame a guy for trying." I cock my head towards her. "You're pretty fucking gorgeous."

"And if I had a nickel every time you've probably used that line on a girl." She scoffs, rebuffing my compliment.

I'm not going to bother trying to convince her. I get it. Why would she believe me? I'm a fucking rock star who can have my pick of any women I want on any given night. And this isn't me being a smug, cocky bastard – it's just a fact.

She knows this and trying to change her opinion of me would be wasted breath. Instead, I shrug. "It's true. Believe me, or don't."

She shifts from one foot to another, her gaze darting around before finding mine. "So, um, is there somewhere that I can wait? Where I won't be in the way?"

She looks so damn innocent, and nice, and so unlike all

the other girls who've found their way into my room. I realize I don't want her to leave. Even if it's not to share the bed with me. She's piqued my curiosity. Not only that, if she goes downstairs and Mikey finds her, he's definitely going to try and sink his claws into her.

Chapter Three
Lily

Sympathy for the Devil
Rolling Stones

"It's fine." His hand drags through his chestnut locks, his eyes finding mine. "You can hang out here while you wait."

"Really?" I can't disguise my surprise. He seemed to want nothing more than for me to leave a few minutes ago.

"Really." He stands, his arms raising above his head in a long stretch before addressing me again. "But I have a condition."

"Of course you do." I scoff. "Let me guess? It involves me taking my clothes off?"

He scratches at the long stubble on his chin, a wisp of a smile on display. "I think you've made it perfectly clear *that's* off the table. But my request does involve the bed."

I cross my arms, arching a brow. "Go on then, what is it?"

"I'm fucking beat." His lips scrunch up as if admitting this was painful. "If I promise to keep my hands off, is it okay if I just crash on the bed? Whatever side you want is yours, but I need some damn sleep."

"Oh." Not at all what I was expecting. But now that he's brought it up, it's hard not to notice the dark circles shadowing his eyes. "You want to go to bed." I surmise out loud. "I can just find somewhere else to wait."

"Probably not as safe out there as you think." He eyes dart in the direction of the door. "Believe it or not, I'm the nice one in the bunch." He nods at the bed. "Seriously, it's fine if you want to hang here. This bed is huge. More than enough room for the two of us."

He sits on the end of and toes off the boots he's wearing, each one thudding to the floor as they drop. He twists to face me. "Preference on a side?"

I shake my head. "Nope. I'm fine right here if you're okay with that."

"Yep." He stands, shifting his gaze to the bathroom. "Just gonna go take care of business."

"Uh, yeah, okay." Not sure he had to explain that situation, but maybe he's trying to make sure I'm not freaked out by any sudden movement. Who knows at this point. Which is turning into one of the strangest nights of my life.

I'm about to share a bed with a legitimate rock god and not because we're going to have sex. Bri is never going to believe me, and then when she finds out, she's going to murder me for not doing the deed.

The door clicks open and he strolls out a second after, my mouth gaping wide. He's naked, minus a very fitted pair of boxer briefs and while, Oh. My. God. does he look amazing, I was not expecting this. "Um, guess you aren't shy?" I can feel my face heating and hate that his practically naked form is making me blush.

"Don't get your panties in a bunch." He tugs back the blankets on the bed to slide under them. "I told you; I need sleep. I'm not wearing my clothes to bed just to make things a little less awkward for you."

I sit in stunned silence for a moment because, he's not wrong. He is letting me hang out in his room. Why should he have to make adjustments for my comfort?

"Sorry," I mumble an apology. "Just wasn't expecting that."

He rolls over so he's facing me, propping his head up under his hand. "Can I ask you something?"

"Okay…"

"What the hell is your name?" He grins, and it's a smile so wide, so natural, his eyes sparkling with a mischief and an ease I hadn't experienced yet. "I mean, if we're in bed together, I should at least know that much about you."

"It's Lily." I offer with a smile. "Lilith actually, but everyone calls me Lily."

He chuffs, a small chuckle escaping. "Well, isn't that interesting?"

"Why?" My curiosity piqued.

"I'm Luc." He shifts so he's sitting, the sheet pooling at his waist as he rests his back against the padded headboard. My attention shifts to his bare chest. His perfectly defined abs.

I realize I'm staring and snap my gaze back up to his face, which is of course, sporting a smug smile as he continues. "Lucifer. And my brother's name is Michael."

I respond with a blank stare waiting for more, but he doesn't say anything, so I go there. "And why is this interesting?"

"You seriously don't know the story of Lucifer and Lilith? The Archangel Michael? Heaven and Hell?" His brow shoots up in disbelief.

My head swings back and forth in slow motion. "Not a church girl. I mean, obviously I know about God, Moses, Jesus, angels, the devil and all that crap."

"Did you know that Lucifer *is* the devil?"

"Say what?" I sit up straighter, seeing him in a whole new light, one that seems kind of appropriate in retrospect.

"Okay, I'm going to keep this as simple as possible and give you the cliff notes version of Lucifer."

"I'm sure you don't need to dumb it down for me." I inform him on a huff.

"It's not that." He gives a slight shake of his head. "If you read the bible, there's actually very little mention of Lucifer. But there is a ton of mythological lore around him, Lilith, and Michael. It's just easier to give you the highlights."

"Okay." I nod in consent. "Cliff notes version it is."

He pulls his bottom lip between his teeth, his head shaking slightly as he chuffs. "You are such a Lilith."

I arch a single brow, blinking in confusion.

"Stubborn. Defiant. Proud." He pauses. "Just a couple of the descriptions used about her in stories."

"I am not-"

"See?" He wags a finger in the air between us. "Case in point. Defiant." He snorts, crossing his arms over his chest as he begins. "Lucifer, and Michael are often referred to as two of the most powerful angels, if not most favored, to God. But Lucifer becomes a little too full of himself and believes he's greater than God, and ends up leading a rebellion against him. Michael is the archangel who leads the heavenly forces against Lucifer during the rebellion, defeating him, and ultimately casts him down into what's now known as Hell. That's how Lucifer came to be known as the devil or Satan."

"Where does Lilith play into all of this?" I wonder out loud.

"Lilith was actually created to be Adam's wife before Eve. But she never loved Adam, and didn't want to listen or obey him. Because of this, Eve was created, and Lilith was freed from her commitment to Adam. She was described as being a rebellious female demon, helping Lucifer in his rebellion against God by giving him her children to use in his army."

"Were Lucifer and Lilith in love?" I shift, turning my body toward his.

He shrugs. "It depends on what interpretation you read. There are many. When he was in Heaven, Lucifer was known as the Morning Star, while Lilith was known as the Goddess of the Night. Together they represented light and dark. Good and evil. Their relationship was described as fiery and intense. But because they were cast into hell, their bond was tested endless times as others tried to tear them apart. It's said their devotion endured through the ages, proving that true love and passion knows no boundaries, even in the darkest of places."

"I don't get it." I muse out loud.

"What's not to get?" His forehead wrinkling as his eyes narrow, a hand reaching up to scratch at the scruff under his chin.

"Why would your parents name you what they did? Lucifer and Michael were enemies."

He shrugs. "We asked my parents the same thing when we learned about the tale."

"And?" I lift my hand, motioning for him to continue.

"It depends on who you ask. My mom says one thing, and my dad another." He fingers the edge of the sheet pooled at his waist. "She claims she wasn't familiar with the story, and just liked the individual names. But my dad says that her pregnancy with me was pure hell, so she thought Lucifer would be a fitting name, while her pregnancy with Mikey was the complete opposite, thus named him Michael."

"Do you think it's true?" I gape at him, wondering if a mother would actually name her child after the devil.

"Who knows." His gaze finds mine. "My parents divorced about ten years ago, and not under the best of circumstances, so they don't tend to say anything nice about each other anymore."

"That sucks." My brow scrunching as I frown. "I'm sorry."

"It is what it is." He shrugs, sliding his body down the length of the bed, his head resting on the pillow. "Gonna go to sleep now." He reaches for the switch on the lamp beside the bed. "Don't want you to think I'm being rude, but I'm beat."

"Thank you for letting me stay." I rush out, genuinely grateful and a little surprised, to be offered temporary sanctuary in his room.

"Let's get one thing clear; I'm keeping my hands to myself because I said I would. Not because I want to." The lamp clicks off, the glow of the city seeping into the room, casting just enough light to keep the room from total darkness. "Don't mistake discipline for lack of interest, Kitten."

My heart skips a beat at his response, a fleeting thought crossing my mind that maybe I wouldn't mind if he wasn't so disciplined.

Chapter Four
Luc

How Soon Is Now
The Smiths

I BLINK, my head a bit fuzzy as my brain switches from sleep to awake. I slept hard. I raise my arms and stretch, rolling over onto my back, freezing when I realize Lily's still in the bed with me. I glance at the clock. It's almost eight. I'm surprised she's still here.

I turn onto my side so I can get a closer look at her. I'm less than six inches from her now. Sometime during the night, she must have slipped under the covers because they are now over her body.

Her face is completely relaxed. I take in the spattering of freckles again that are on display across her cheeks and the bridge of her nose. They make her look like a young girl, instead of the young woman I know she is. Did she tell me her age last night? I can't remember.

There's a thick strand of hair that's fallen across her forehead and over her eyes. I lift my hand to brush the locks off her face and behind her ear. Her lids flutter open, a small smile lifting the corners of her mouth as her eyes connect and lock with mine.

My gaze shifts to her lips, the bottom one now clenched between her teeth, and then back to her eyes. I pause again as I absorb how light they are - like the blue color you see reflected in an ice cube - crisp and vibrant.

She blinks, effectively ending the staring contest we seem to be having, my attention diverting to the perfect cupid's bow below her nose.

I lean forward, pausing just a breath away from her, seeking silent consent before brushing my lips against hers as I close the gap between us. The tiniest whimper sounds as I swipe my tongue against the opening of her mouth, our kiss intensifying in pressure.

I thread my fingers through her hair at her temple to tilt her head back, releasing her mouth, dragging my tongue up the column of her neck before claiming her lips again.

A moan vibrates against me as she shifts her entire body into mine, not an inch of space between us now as her arms snake around my neck, fingers grasping onto the hair at my nape. We kiss each other like we're starving. Our teeth clacking together as a result of the frantic push and pull of our bodies against each other.

I slide a hand under her tank top, grazing my hand up her ribs until I find the peak of her nipple. I roll it between my fingers, her back arching into my hold, her mouth falling open around mine on a gasp.

Her hands loosen the hold they have on my neck,

breaking away from me, my brow immediately pulling into a furrow until I see that she's tugging on the hem of her shirt to yank it over her head. I grin. I can't help myself. Her tits are amazing. Smallish, but full.

I don't hesitate at the offering and slide down her body, my tongue flicking the hard, raised bud before I suck it between my lips. I roll her onto her back, and worship her breasts one at a time, her fingers tethered to my skull as I do.

I skim lower, pressing wet kisses to her taut stomach, dragging my tongue over her belly button, stopping when I reach the waist of her skirt.

She lifts her hips, helping me push the fabric over her hips and down her legs, her underwear going with it. I glance up, eyes locking with hers, making sure she's okay with this. She nods, her fingers pinching one of her nipples, her lip locked in her teeth again. My dick turns to stone at the sight. She's fucking fire and I want nothing more than to burn.

I lower myself between her legs, gliding a hand up the inside of her thigh until I reach the apex of her legs. I swipe my thumb between her folds, already wet, then press against her clit. Her back bows off the bed as she clutches onto my strands again, panting loud.

I descend further, inhaling deeply, savoring her musky scent, sweet and salty at the same time. I lean in and claim the bundle of nerves with a sweep of my tongue. Her taste explodes in my mouth, sweeter than I expected.

My cock throbs against the material of my boxers, so I work to push them off with one hand. It bobs free, releasing some of the tension, but alleviating none of the want surging through me.

She so fucking wet, her ass wiggling under me as I lick

her from top to bottom, my hands locked on her thighs, spreading her legs wide. I release one hand to slide a finger inside her, and pump it slowly back and forth.

She releases a guttural moan, and I smile as I continue to lap up her juices. I can feel her starting to build toward her orgasm but I'm not ready for this to end yet, so I glide my finger out of her and pepper kisses back up her body.

Our mouths fuse when I reach her lips, my cock aching as it lands between her legs. She spreads them and without hesitation, I thrust inside of her in one shove.

Both of our mouths fall open on a gasp at the welcomed intrusion. She's so fucking tight, it takes a second for me to adjust to her walls squeezing around my dick.

I wait a second and then move my hips back just a fraction before pushing them forward again. I do this again and again, each time pulling back a little further, until our waists are thrusting against each other, her nails digging into my back. Hot breaths pant out of her into my ear, my elbows resting on either side of her, our foreheads pressed together.

I sense it before I feel her start to convulse around my cock; heat surrounding my shaft as I follow her over the edge, my release crashing over me, my vision black for a moment at the intensity of it. We clasp onto each other, our breaths huffing out of us, our bodies pulsing as we both climb to heaven and then float back to earth.

After a moment, I roll off of her onto my back, pulling her body into my side to wrap against mine. I realize, as I lay beside her panting, that we haven't said a single word to each other, yet it's the most connected I've felt with anyone in more time than I can remember.

It also dawns on me that I didn't put a condom on. *Fuck.*

How do I broach this without coming off like a complete asshole?

"Are you okay?"

I feel her head slide up and down on my shoulder as she nods. "Uh-huh."

"That happened so quickly I forgot to put a condom on." I just throw it out there because it needs to be said. I have to take accountability for my complete lack of responsibility.

Her head pops up. "Oh shit. We did forget that, didn't we?"

"We did." I frown. "I'm sorry. Got lost in the moment."

"I can grab a Plan B from the drugstore later." She hangs her head a moment before dragging her gaze back to mine. "Do I need to worry about getting tested or anything?"

"Do I?" I counter.

"Touche." She cocks her head, flashing me a quick smile. "I haven't had sex in about five months, but it was with someone pretty serious, and safe."

"I'm not volunteering when I last had sex, but I promise, it's always safe." I grimace as I continue. "Not sure where my head was at this time."

"Ah, between my legs?" She blushes a deep red at her own joke.

"Yeah, good point." I chuckle. "I can have one of my people go grab that pill for you if you want?"

"No, no." She shakes her head. "I can do it later. It's not a big deal."

"As long as you're sure."

"Don't worry. I'm not secretly trying to knock myself up with your baby." She shifts to a sitting position, pulling the sheet up to cover the front of her body.

"Didn't even cross my mind." I lie, because let's face it,

there are some crazy fucking chicks out there that might try to do just that.

This girl though, she definitely isn't that. She's an enigma, and one that's got me curious. She's a puzzle that I want to solve. "Spend the day with me."

The words are out in the atmosphere before I even realize what I'm saying, I think shocking me more than her.

Chapter Five
Lily

Cover Me in Sunshine
P!nk

"WHAT?" My spine stiffens as I sit up straight.

"If you aren't already doing something." He shifts, pressing his back against the padding of the headboard, the sheet pooling at his waist.

"Why would you want to spend the day with me? And don't you have a concert later?" I spit out. My brain not only reeling at his invitation, but at the fact I just had sex with an almost complete stranger, who happens to be the lead singer of one of the most popular rock bands in the world. *Whoa.*

He cocks his head, crossing his arms over his torso, his lips pursing before he speaks. "You're different."

"Than what?" I ask.

"Than everyone else." He states matter of fact.

"And that's a good thing?" I question.

"I've spent the last three months on the road with the guys in the band, our roadies, our crew, all the people making sure we get to the right place at the right time. Every single one of them either kissing or kicking our asses. So, yeah, it's a good thing."

He pauses, scratching at the scruff lining his chin, something that seems to be a nervous tic with him. "You could give two shits who I am or what I do. I kind of like the fact that you aren't intimidated by me in the least."

"Says who?" I reject his observation with wide eyes. "I'm completely intimidated by you."

"Nah." He shrugs. "Now if I was Keith Urban, maybe that would be different."

"He's too old." I tease in return. "Morgan Wallen, however."

He flashes a smile that mirrors mine. "So, what do you say?"

"About spending the day with you?" I repeat it to make sure I actually heard the original request correctly.

"Yes, about spending the day with me." He reiterates, smiling broadly. "I don't have to be at the arena until around seven. Let's go do something."

I stare at him, running different scenarios in my head as to how and where this day could possibly lead to. "I have conditions."

"Of course you do." He chuffs with a shake of his head. "Tell me."

"Rule number one, no personal stuff." I pause for effect and to take in his reaction. "Let's keep it light and easy. We spend the day together but we don't do the thing where we pretend we're going to see each other again after this, or that we're going to ride off into the sunset together. Let's just have fun. No expectations. No disappointments." I fold my arms as I finish up, proud of myself at this practical suggestion.

"But what if I want to see you again?" A single brow raises.

"Tonight's your last show here, right? Aren't you leaving tomorrow for the next stop?" I defend, knowing full well the band is leaving because Bri wouldn't stop talking about how she had to *get* Dean last night since the band was only in town a couple days.

"Yeah, but I have a jet." He throws out, smirking like he's talking about having a Honda.

"Of course you do." I quip, unable to hide my own smile.

"Fine." He leans forward, wrapping a hand around the back of my neck pulling me forward to press a kiss on my lips. "I agree to your terms."

"No personal stuff. No expectations." I repeat.

"Got it." He salutes, a smirk breaking across his face.

"I'm going to need to go to my apartment to change though. Can we do that?" As I ask the question, I search around the bed for my scattered clothes.

"We can do that."

I watch him stand and stretch, the sheet left behind like an afterthought. No shame, no hesitation. God, he was trouble. But even knowing this didn't put a damper on my curiosity about him. Maybe a little trouble was exactly what I needed.

"I'm going to take a quick shower, then we can head out." He rakes a hand through his already tousled hair as he strolls in the direction of the bathroom.

"Sounds good." I gape at his naked ass, marveling at its perfection and the fact I had my hands on it just a short time ago.

He shuts the door behind him, and I scramble out of the bed to toss my clothes on while the coast is clear. I'm not ashamed of my body at all, but I might be a little shy about exposing myself to him again so soon.

I snatch my phone off the bedside table and sigh in relief that it's not dead. I haven't charged it since yesterday morning.

I silenced it when Luc shut the light off last night, not wanting it to wake him up if Bri texted. I scan my notifications and open the six texts I received from her while I was sleeping.

3:30 a.m."Hey girl. Wya?"
3:47 a.m."Should I be worried you aren't answering?"
4:01 a.m. "Okay, going to crash in Dean's room for a little bit. Text me!"
6:30 a.m. "WYA??? Now I am worried. Text me bitch."
7:01 a.m. "Drop me a fucking pin so I know you're alive."
8:07 a.m. "You better be dead, cause if you're not I'm going to kill you when I find out where you are."

Fuuuuuck. She's gonna be so pissed at me. I find her number and hit send, only one ring sounding before her voice is screeching through the phone. "Where in the fuckity fuck are you? I've been freaking out for hours!"

"I'm sorry!" I wince as I ramble out my excuse. "I found an empty room and fell asleep."

"You *just fell asleep somewhere?*" Her tone incredulous and very annoyed.

"I'm serious! There was an empty room, I was exhausted, I crashed. Nothing happened."

There's a loud huff through the phone. "Nothing

happened? So, you didn't get kidnapped, drunk-dial an ex, or join a cult? Because those were all real options on the list I made this morning while I was worried sick about you."

She is going to kill me when I tell her the truth. *If I tell her the truth.* She may never let me live this one down.

"No cults. No exes. Just...sleep. Swear." I cross my fingers as I spout the lie.

"You're sketchy as hell right now. I can *hear* it. What aren't you telling me?"

My heart rate ratchets up a notch as I realize my best friend knows me inside and out, and can tell I might be bull-shitting her, but I'm all in now, so I keep going. "Nothing! I'm just tired. I'm good."

"Mm-hmm." She murmurs, not buying what I'm selling for one minute. "Sure. I'm putting you on high-level best friend probation until I can look you in the eyes to sniff out the truth."

I wait a second to see if she's done with her rant, then chime in with my next lie.

"I'm heading home now to try and catch up on some of the sleep I missed. Are you still at the hotel?"

"I'm home." She lets out a little growl of frustration. "And thanks to you, I barely got a wink of sleep because I couldn't stop pacing the floor waiting for you to text me."

I cringe and attempt another apology. "I really am sorry."

"I know, I know." I can hear her take a sip of something. "I'm caffeinating up and then heading to work. I have a shift at the restaurant today. I'm on until six."

"Okay, maybe meet up later then?" I suggest, trying to redeem myself.

"Let's meet for brunch tomorrow. At our regular place?

I'm pretty sure all I'm going to want to do after being up all night and now all day, is crash."

"It's a date."

I grin, relief flooding through me that she seems to have already forgiven me. "Ten-thirty?"

"Perfect." She makes a kissing sound. "Bye, bitch."

The line disconnects between us just as Luc walks out of the bathroom, a towel secured around his waist, steam trailing behind him.

"Everything kosher?"

I nod. "Yep, just had to check in with Bri." I clarify for him who she is. "The friend I was here with last night that hooked up with Dean."

"I remember." His mouth crooks up in a wicked grin. "Did you tell her about me?"

"None of your business." I shoot back at him. "Nothing personal, remember?"

"Oh, so we've started the game?" His head angling as he drops the towel, and prowls in my direction.

"Is this a game?" I take two tentative steps away from him, my back hitting the wall, stalling my escape.

"Well, you did assign rules." He reaches me before I have time to change course, his arms coming up to rest on either side of me, effectively caging me in.

His breath smells minty as he leans his body into mine. "I think it's only fair I get to assign some as well."

"Okay…" I manage to mumble, my eyes transfixed on his, their color mesmerizing me all over again.

"Rule two, I kiss you when I want. If you don't want it, you say it. Otherwise, it's happening. Rule three, wear a skirt. Not for them. For me." His gaze skims down my body, then back up, his simmering look making it clear he won't argue on this point. "Rule four, no makeup, I want the freckles. And rule five, I'm going to fuck you at least one more time." He pauses, his eyes staring directly into mine. "Probably twice."

Yep, face is definitely red, my bottom lip now clenched between my teeth. His thumb is suddenly under my chin, tilting it up as he angles his mouth to mine before capturing my lip in a gentle nip, pulling it free from my hold.

"Stop destroying this beautiful mouth." His tongue darts out to swipe against the tender skin, and I swear, my knees almost buckle.

"Last rule-" His hand slides up to caress my cheek, fingers sliding to the back of my head as he rests his forehead to mine. "No matter what happens, you promise you'll give me your number when we say goodbye."

I go to speak but he shakes his head and keeps talking. "No excuses. No more fucking rules. I can guarantee one day with you won't be enough."

Holy shit. Is this guy for real?

My heart is hammering in my chest and I wonder if he can feel it. He is not at all what I expected after his cocky act last night during the party.

I spit out the first thing that pops into my head, I'm sure spurred by what I witnessed. "I'm not doing drugs."

He barks out a laugh as he takes a step back, his hold on me releasing. "Yeah, I kind of figured."

He smiles then. And it's warm and kind and everything I know is going to fuck with my head and heart later. "You're the only drug I need today, Kitten."

This time, when he calls me the pet name he seems to have so fondly assigned to me, I don't mind one damn bit.

Chapter Six
Luc

Devil Inside
INXS

I HAVE no idea what I'm doing with this damn girl, but I can't seem to bring myself to say goodbye to her. I'm a little shocked at my own actions but fuck it, I'm rolling with it because it's the best I've felt in months.

She makes me feel normal again. She doesn't seem to give two shits that I'm famous. I love that she tries to take the lead, but is such a natural at being led.

We're in an Uber on the way to her apartment, both of us quiet, seemingly lost in our own thoughts. I reach over and draw her hand against my palm. Her mouth pulls up into a smile, her fingers folding over mine, fusing them together as she glances over at me.

It's September in Las Vegas, and still goddamn stifling out, but I only had jeans in my room, so I'm in those and a t-shirt. I had chucks, thank God, so at least I didn't have to put my boots on.

I threw on a baseball cap and sunglasses, not sure how much of a disguise they'll act as, but I'm hoping I can get through the day without being recognized.

A few minutes later, we pull into a complex, every damn building looking exactly like the other, the car pulling up to one somewhere in the middle of the maze.

We get out, thank the driver, and she leads me in between two buildings and up a flight of exterior stairs. I remove my sunglasses and slide them into the front of my shirt collar.

She pauses in front of a door then turns to look at me. "It might be messy. I obviously wasn't expecting to bring-" She scans me from head to toe before continuing. "-you here."

"I live in hotel rooms six months a year, I'm sure it's fine." I reassure her. I could care less if she's a messy Marvin or neat as a pin. It doesn't fucking matter. It's her I'm interested in, not her housekeeping skills.

"Okay, I'm just warning you." She spins back around and punches a code into the lock on the knob and pushes the door open, her voice raising an octave as she calls out. "Teddy Bear, I'm home."

What the fuck?

Before I can ask the question, a fluffy furball streaks into the room, purring so loud it sounds like a motorcycle engine, stopping when it reaches her legs.

He's cute as hell, but I'm hoping he's the only one. If three more cats show up, I'm out. I did not sign up for single, crazy cat lady.

She bends down and scoops him up, planting several kisses against his forehead as she turns to me. "This is Teddy," warmth beaming from her. "He's my roommate."

I scratch his head, his purring intensifying as he bumps

his skull up into my hand. "He's definitely a friendly little dude."

"Yep." She plops another kiss on his head before placing him back on the floor. "He's a good boy."

She sweeps a look around her place then glances back at me. "Okay, I'm going to take a really quick shower."

She points towards a living room area. "You can hang in there, watch something if you want? Help yourself to anything in the fridge." She frowns as her focus shifts in that direction. "It's probably pretty sparse. I don't cook very much."

"I'm good." I wave her off. "Go do your thing." I reach down to swipe the cat out from under her legs and cradle him in my arms. "I'll hang out with this guy."

She stares at me a moment, her eyes shifting from the cat in my arms and then back up to my face, wearing an expression I can't read, before she finally nods. "Okay. I'll be quick."

"Take your time." I call to her as she scurries down a hallway off the kitchen and into a doorway on the right. I saunter around the open space of her apartment, the cat completely content hanging out against my chest.

She's got framed pictures on the counter in the kitchen, one with her friend from last night, and another with a larger group of girlfriends. I wander into the living room area, and browse the list of titles to books stacked up in multiple rows under one of the windows.

Some of them I recognize, some of them I don't. She's got classics mixed in with Stephen King, mixed in with E.L. James, mixed in with Ken Follett. She's diversified; I'll give her that.

She's got an actual stereo, with a record player, a crate of albums beside it. This definitely has me interested. I place the cat on the couch and go back over to the crate.

I slide out a stack of albums and start browsing through them. Patsy Cline, George Strait, Clint Black, Garth Brooks and Keith Urban. I knew she was an Urban fan! There's Johnny Cash, The Beatles, Dolly Parton, The Eagles and Carrie Underwood.

I guess she wasn't kidding when she said she was a die-hard country fan, but she's obviously in touch with some of the classics. I'm going to do my damndest today to get her to like one of my songs. I chuckle, then put the albums back where I found them.

The cat's curled up in a ball on the couch, so I go sit next to him, absently patting him as I grab my phone to kill some time. I pull my cap off and set it on the couch beside the cat. A short time later, I hear footsteps pattering in my direction, so I shove my phone in my pocket as I stand, my breath catching when she comes into view.

I feel my cheeks lift as I stare at her in approval. She's wearing a sundress. One of those with the cute little straps that are tied at the top of her shoulders, the skirt falling to mid-thigh. It's white with some kind of pretty blue flowers scattered all over.

The kicker though? She's wearing those frilly edged bobby socks again, but this time with a pair of denim-colored chucks. Her face is free of make-up, her hair flowing in loose waves around her shoulders. She's fucking adorable.

I amble over to her, her eyes popping wide when I grip her waist to push her back against the wall.

"You followed the rules."

Now that I'm next to her, her scent invades my senses. I

inhale deeply, dragging my nose along the column of her neck.

It's sweet and exotic, with a hint of something musky beneath. It clings to her like an invisible aura, wrapping around me, making everything else in the room fade away. It's like breathing in the night air just after a storm, fresh, bold, and completely addictive. "You smell fucking amazing."

I reach her mouth and press my lips to hers, consuming any response she may have been about to provide. The kiss deepens, my lips no longer just pressing against hers but claiming them with a slow, deliberate intensity.

I slide my hands to her neck, tilting her head, getting lost in the feel of her, wanting, no, needing more. So much more. I breathe her in, let it drown me. I trace the line of her mouth with my lips, soft and teasing, before plunging back into the kiss, devouring her.

Her breath hitches against mine, which spurs me even harder. My heart pounds, every beat syncing to the rhythm of our kiss. It isn't just the taste of her. Something deeper pulls at me. The way she fits against me. The way she makes everything burn brighter, hotter.

The tension between us builds, pressing against me in ways that make everything else disappear. This kiss isn't just about desire, it's about something rawer, something that feels dangerously close to losing control.

But right now, the control is mine, and I'm going to make sure she feels every second of it in each stolen breath turning this kiss into something far more than I ever expected.

"I want you." I growl, my tongue tracing the shell of her ear before I nip her neck.

"Yes." She gasps, her hands wrenching the clasp of my belt

undone, shoving my pants down far enough for my cock to spring loose.

I reach under the hem of her dress until I find the top of her underwear and yank them off her. She steps out of them as I hoist her onto my hips, slamming her against the wall, my cock sliding against her heat.

"Hold on to me." I command, letting go of her with one hand so I can guide myself to her center. I plunge into her with one thrust, the heat of her swallowing my dick whole.

"Fuck." I groan, her fingers clawing onto my shoulders as she grinds her hips into mine. "You are so goddamn tight."

"Don't stop." She mewls, her lips moving against mine.

"I haven't even started, baby." I grind out, giving her what she asks for. I angle my hips and drive my cock as deep as I can, her shoulders and head thudding against the wall with each shove.

"Yes, yes." She chants with every buck of my body, her arms and legs locked around me, choking on to me, the thin material of our clothing the only thing between our bodies.

After several minutes her channel starts to pulse around my shaft. "I'm coming." Her breath hot against my face as she pants her status.

"Yes. Fuck, yes. Come all over my cock, Kitten." I order, my knees going weak as her pussy tightens around my dick, a low moan escaping from her before her teeth bite into my shoulder.

I wait as long as I can for her to finish, then pull out of her, grip my dick, wet and slippery, and pump myself twice, cum spurting onto her bare leg. I slam one hand on the wall beside her head to keep from collapsing, stars exploding under my lids as I let out a rumbling groan from deep inside of me.

I open my eyes slowly, my head resting against my arm, and look over at her. She's breathing as hard as me, her head leaning back against the wall, eyes closed.

"Are you okay?" I wheeze out between breaths.

"Yep." She nods, her lids opening to meet my gaze. "Are you?"

"I'm fucking great." I jut one side of my mouth up in a grin. "Never better."

"Guess you were serious about those rules." She jokes, laughing lightly.

"One for one so far." I wink, then straighten, releasing my hold on the wall.

"Let me get you something to clean that up." I glance down at my release dripping down her leg.

"There's wash clothes in that closet at the end of the hall." She points in the direction I should go.

"On it."

I stroll away, my dick, now soft, bobbing limply against my lower waist. I grab two of the small towels, then stride into the kitchen, running them under hot water. I squeeze out the excess, then wipe my dick with one, as I beeline back to her.

I bend down, and starting just above her sock, drag the warm cloth up the inside of her leg, cleaning off the result of our encounter. I stop short at the top of her leg, not sure if this is a little too personal, so peer up at her for permission to continue.

She stares down at me, that goddamn lip between her teeth again, her chest rising and falling rapidly. She doesn't say no, so I flatten my hand under the cloth and wipe her pussy, spreading my fingers as I go, applying light pressure.

A gasp tumbles from her, her pussy contracting under my

touch, my dick twitching at her response. Jesus Christ with this girl. She looks fucking sweeter than an angel, but definitely has a touch of the devil inside her.

I finish, then stand. I lean forward, and using my teeth, pluck her lip from her grasp, mumbling against her. "I thought I told you to stop that."

"Sorry." She responds meekly.

"Where can I put these?" I motion to the soiled linens in my hand.

"Here." She takes them from me before turning in the direction of the hall. "I think I need to freshen up again."

I chuff. "Not sorry."

She turns, looking over her shoulder, a sexy little grin on her face, as she saunters down the hall. "Neither am I."

Chapter Seven
Lily

Bloody Valentine
(Acoustic Version)
Machine Gun Kelly

Who am I? And what in the hell did I just do?

I stare at my reflection in the mirror above the sink, my cheeks flushed from the pounding I just got in my hallway.

I don't do shit like this!

I splash some cold water over my face, then dab it dry. I walk into my adjoining bedroom and snag a fresh pair of panties from the top drawer of my dresser. I pull them on over my sneakers and under the skirt of my dress. My third pair in less than twelve hours. At this rate, my underwear drawer will need a restock and my self-control definitely needs some reigning in.

Maybe I should back out of this day with Luc before things get even crazier. I mean, who am I kidding? This guy is a bonafide rockstar and if I think I am even close to being in the same league with him, I might as well also believe he's going to even remember my name in a month.

I do not live in a fantasy land. I'm a sensible girl and make sensible decisions. Until today apparently.

Shit.

Should I call Bri and get her advice? I didn't tell her about this earlier because I knew exactly what her reaction would be. I didn't want to deal with that, but now I'm second guessing every decision I'm making.

There's a soft knock at the bathroom door. I grit my teeth, walk over and lean against it letting out a long sigh.

"I can hear you over thinking in there." He states softly. "Are you okay?"

I push back off the door, shake my head toward the sky then yank the door open. He's standing there, his hands in his pockets, shoulders hunched, those whiskey eyes locking onto mine in question.

"Is this a normal thing for you?" I blurt out.

His brow shoots up, one hand escaping his pocket to rake through his hair as he chuckles. "Which part?"

"Oh my God." I sputter, forcing myself around him as I plow back out to the living room where I don't feel so claustrophobic.

"Hey." A light grip surrounds my forearm to spin me around, his free hand wrapping around my other arm to hold me in place. "You freaking out?"

I nod frantically; my eyes wide. "Uh-huh."

"Stop." He releases one arm and raises that hand to my face to caress my cheek. "Take a breath."

I draw in a deep inhale through my nose, my chest expanding, then release it slowly, never breaking eye contact with him.

"I'm just a guy. And I met a girl I actually want to spend some time with." His thumb sweeps over the skin on my face. "That's it. We aren't doing anything wrong."

"But-" I start to protest, which he promptly stops by covering my mouth with his. He breaks away after a few seconds.

"No buts." He surprises me by sliding his arms around me, enveloping me in a hug. "Stop overthinking this. Let's just go."

I lift my arms from my side to wrap them around his back. My head rests against his chest where I can hear the steady thump of his heartbeat. It calms me. Reassures me. It's slow and steady, not the slightest bit erratic.

I loosen my hold to step back from him, his forearms adjusting so they're resting atop my shoulders. I raise my head until my eyes meet his.

"Where do you want to go?" I ask sheepishly.

"I could eat." He suggests on a shrug.

I think about this for a minute, an idea springing to mind. "Are you hungry or starving?"

"Hungry."

"Okay, I know a place." I offer a small smile. "I think it'll be perfect. It's quiet and out of the way so hopefully no one will know who you are."

"Sounds great." He steps back and slides his phone out of his pocket. "Want me to call us an Uber?"

"I can drive." I assure him, walking to the hook where my keys are hanging. "Let me just grab my purse."

"You sure you don't mind driving?" He strides over to the couch, swiping his ball cap to pull it onto his head, the bill facing backwards. *Jesus Christ that's hot.* "I can always call one of my drivers."

I pause, my brow rising in disbelief. "What happened to you're just a guy? A regular guy."

"Got it." He back pedals. "No car. You drive."

"Much better." I roll my eyes, smiling. "It takes about forty-five minutes to get there, but I promise it'll be worth it."

"I call DJ." He blurts, a wicked grin lighting up his face. "I'm going to get you to like at least one of my songs before the end of the day."

"Good luck." I chuckle, but more than happy to let him try.

I don't dislike rock music, or any other kind of music for that matter. I just prefer country. I love the song writing, the stories most of them contain.

I lead him out the door, making sure it's locked behind me, and then head in the direction of my car. I click the button on the remote to unlock the doors, a loud chuff of laughter sounding next to me.

"You've got to be fucking kidding me."

I cock my head, not understanding his reaction. "What?"

"This?" He points to my car. "*This is your car*? A fucking Hellcat?" He shakes his head, chuckling again. "You are full of surprises, Kitten."

"It was my dad's. I always loved it." I open the driver's side door to slide in, as he does the same on the passenger side. "He passed away a few years ago and my mom gave it to me. She said having it in the driveway reminded her too much of him."

"Shit." He frowns. "I'm sorry about your dad. What happened?"

"Nope." I insert the key to start the engine before I reply, the sweet hum of the engine making me smile. "Too personal. Breaks rule number one."

"Fair enough." He cocks his head. "Do I get to know where you're bringing me?"

I put the car in reverse and back out of my parking space, then steer out of the complex towards the highway. "A place called Canyon Restaurant. It's up on Mt. Charleston, a little bit outside of town. It's gorgeous up there. You won't even believe you're in Vegas anymore."

"That sounds perfect." He grins broadly, sliding his sunglasses on. "By the way, that dress is gorgeous on you."

I start to chew on my bottom lip in an attempt to hide my smile, but stop short, letting the corners of my mouth lift instead, my insides warming at his compliment. "Thank you."

"So, let's see what I can teach you about music in the next half-hour." He presses a few buttons on the screen centered in the dash until he finds the Bluetooth settings.

A second later his phone is out and he's pairing it to the car. He turns his head, a wide grin lifting his cheeks. "You ready?"

"Hit me with your best shot." I gun the engine as we turn onto the 11, traffic finally breaking up.

He hits the play button and a moment later chords of a guitar strum gently, a gravelly voice sounding over the speakers a second later. The melody is slow, the lyrics actually clear.

I listen, absorbing the message of the song. My pulse quickening when I translate it's about a guy who seems to have fallen for a girl who was supposed to be anything but a permanent stain on his heart.

I sneak a peek at Luc, only to find him staring intently in

my direction, I'm sure to gauge my reaction. He remains silent until the song finishes.

"It's called Bloody Valentine." He volunteers as he glances down at his phone. "There's a faster version, but I like the acoustic one better."

"I like it." I confess, but of course have to throw in some resistance. "It's not exactly what I would classify as a *rock* song."

"Yeah, but it's one of my favorites, so I wanted to play it for you." He clears his throat, staring out the windshield a minute. "It's pretty out here."

"Wait until we get to the top of the mountain." I nod at the stereo. "What else you got for me?"

"Here's one that's definitely rock." He scrolls on his phone a second, a guitar riff, accompanied by some heavy drums exploding over the speakers. He turns it up – loud - and begins to sing along to the words when they start.

I realize immediately it's one of his, and witnessing the pride and passion he exudes as he bellows out the song is breathtaking.

My fingers start tapping of their own accord on the steering wheel, his energy infectious as his head bobs along to the rhythm.

As the last note fades, he shoots me a look, the corners of his mouth curving up like he already knows he's won me over. That grin? It was all confidence, the kind that has my stomach doing flip-flops.

"All right, all right." I concede, unable to contain the smile blooming on my own face. "That wasn't half bad."

And I mean, come on, any guy that has a voice like that is going to make any girl's panties combust.

He throws his arms up, calling out a whoop, declaring

himself a winner. My cheeks lift even higher. He can totally have this victory. He earned it.

"When did you know you wanted to be a singer?" I ask, curious about how he got his start.

"I don't know." His brow scrunches up in thought. "Maybe when I was five or six. My mom jokes that I sang before I could talk."

"Do you play any instruments?"

He shrugs. "Guitar, piano, drums, and I can pluck away on a bass if I need to." He stops, glancing over at me. "Are you okay if I roll the window down a bit?"

"Absolutely." I nod, pushing down the button on my door to lower mine halfway as he does the same.

"I write most of my songs using a piano, then convert the music into a melody on an acoustic guitar for the guys." He shrugs. "Enough about me. What do you do when you aren't sneaking into random guy's rooms at parties?"

A smirk decorates his face, and even though his eyes are covered by his sunglasses, I'm sure they're sparkling with mischief.

"Nope." I shoot a quick glance his way. "Too personal."

"Seriously?" He huffs out. "Is that really fair? You know what I do."

"Uh yeah, because I saw you up on stage last night," I argue. "But if I hadn't, trust me when I tell you, I would have had no idea who you are or what you do if I met you in a crowd."

"Ouch." His hands clutch the area over his heart. "Way to hit a guy where it hurts."

He chuckles. "Not even a hint at what you do? What if I guess? Will you tell me if I get it?"

"I work in the hotel industry." I relent just a little because

I don't see any harm in giving him this tiny bit of information. "That's all you're getting."

"Call girl?" His whole face lights up as he flashes a teasing grin my way.

"Um, definitely not." I smirk, then point to a sign on the side of the road that boasts the restaurant name, using it as a tactic to change the subject. "Almost there."

"Good. I've moved into the starving category." He advises, running a hand over his stomach, which grumbles as if on cue. We both break out laughing.

"Okay, I have one more question for you." Using his index finger, he lowers his sunglasses down the bridge of his nose until I can see his eyes. They skim down the length of my body, stopping where the material of my skirt is pooled around my upper thighs, then back up until he meets my gaze.

"Did you ever put your panties back on?"

I stare straight ahead, blinking like maybe I misheard him. I didn't. My pulse is absolutely *screaming* in my ears now, every nerve in my body suddenly tuned to the heat pulsing between my thighs, and the man responsible for it.

Don't react.

Don't give him the satisfaction.

That smug little chuckle of his is still hanging in the air like smoke, and I swear I feel it curl around my skin. The worst part? I'm not even mad. I should be. He's cocky, shameless, and knows *exactly* how to get under my skin. But instead, I'm sitting here wondering if I should squeeze my legs together, or spread them.

"Luc," I say, my voice strangled and just a little higher than normal.

He doesn't respond, his fingers tapping in time with the

music on the leg of his jeans, like he didn't just ask me one of the most inappropriate, filthy, absolutely soul-snatching questions I've ever been asked in broad daylight.

And then, *then*, he glances over and winks. "Don't worry, Kitten," he warns, keeping his eyes straight ahead. "I'll figure it out later."

Oh. I am in so much trouble.

Chapter Eight
Luc

Lovesong
The Cure

HER CHEEKS FLUSH A DEEP, gorgeous pink. My dick throbs against the constraint of my jeans at the thought of her bare under that little skirt.

If I wasn't so goddamn hungry, I'd already have one hand sliding up her thigh to find out the answer for myself. But I am starving. And, for more than just her, so instead, I shift in my seat, and let a low chuckle roll out of my chest.

She doesn't say anything right away. Just stares out the windshield, stiff and silent like she's trying to act unaffected. But I see it. The way her thighs press together just a little tighter. The way she swallows hard, her jaw locked like she's trying to keep a whole-ass reaction from slipping past her lips. That's not nothing.

And when she finally speaks, *"Luc"*, it's breathy, it's soft, it's just this side of flustered. Music to my fucking ears. I bite back a grin and keep my focus straight ahead, letting the silence stretch out. I want her squirming. I want her wondering what else I'll say. What else I'll do.

Out of the corner of my eye, I catch her glancing at me, like she's checking to see if I'm still watching her.

I am. Of course, I am. It's practically impossible not to.

"We're here." She blurts out as we pull up in front of a hotel entrance. She shifts into park as the car rolls to a stop, a valet driver appearing from the shadows to open her door.

"Checking in?" He inquires, extending a hand to help her out of the car, as I exit on the opposite side.

She wasn't kidding. It's gorgeous here.

"Nope." She takes the ticket he offers. "Going to the restaurant."

"Got it." The valet nods. "See you in a little bit."

She thanks him, walking around the rear of the car to my side. I grab her hand in mine, liking how smooth it is, noting how perfect it feels in mine.

My heart does a little jolt against my rib cage at the real-ization. I'm leaving tomorrow. There is no way I can let myself get attached to this girl. To any girl. My lifestyle just doesn't support that luxury.

Maybe when I decide to stop touring with the band. Besides, I'm only twenty-eight. I'm nowhere near ready to find 'the one' and settle my shit down. *This is not the time to fall in love.*

"You freaking out?" Her fingers clench around mine, pulling me out of my own head.

"What?"

She inclines her head toward our linked fingers. "Your palm just got really sweaty."

I'm glad I have my glasses on so she can't read any truth my eyes might reveal. "It's hot."

I realize it's a shitty excuse the moment the words leave me. Not only are we now at the top of a mountain, we're in the hotel lobby, which is clearly air-conditioned.

"If you say so." She chirps. I know she's letting it slide, so I don't push the issue. She's giving me this one and I'll take it.

We reach a hostess station and she asks for a table outside. It's almost eleven, and we seem to be lucky, catching the restaurant between the breakfast and lunch rush. We're led to a table that's out on a deck, up against a wooden banister. The view is amazing. All I can see are miles and miles of pine trees. Not a single hotel or casino in sight.

"You were right." I pull a chair out for her to sit and then lower myself into the seat beside her. "You would never know The Strip is thirty miles away."

"Told ya." She beams as she accepts the menu from the hostess who informs us our server will be with us shortly. "They have the best bloody Mary's too, if you're interested."

"Vodka for breakfast?" A wide smile breaks across my face. "You are definitely my kind of girl."

She snickers. "The easy kind?"

My expression softens, and I slide my sunglasses off. "I don't think that about you at all." I scoot my chair until it's flush with hers, wanting her to understand I mean it. "I think you're incredible. Smart. Funny. Obviously independent."

I rest my hand on the bare skin of her thigh. "I definitely do not think you're a girl who jumps into bed with people you've just met. Especially someone like me."

"Okay." Her response is quiet, her eyes shifting away, and it feels like she's just telling me what she thinks I want to hear.

"I mean it." I squeeze my fingers around her flesh until her gaze swings back to mine. "I have never, and I do mean never, spent the day with someone after a hookup. You aren't that. You're much more."

Our gazes remain locked, both of us staring into the soul of the other, looking for what, I'm not sure, until we're wrenched back to reality by a chipper voice.

"Sorry to interrupt. You two ready to order?"

"Two bloody Mary's to start." I clip out, not breaking eye contact with Lily, wanting her to feel my full attention is on her, and her alone.

The waitress reads the situation and advises she'll be back with our drinks in a second before scurrying away.

"I'm trying to figure out why the hell a girl like you decided to spend the day with a guy like me." I turn my head away, twisting the cap on my head until the bill is over my eyes, shifting in my seat.

"A girl like me?" She counters, her head tilting as her focus remains on me.

"Good." I state bluntly, scratching at my scruff. "And don't try and deny it. It's what you are. And it's not a diss in the slightest. Girls like you tend to stay away from guys like me."

A grin breaks across her face. "Well, to be fair, I was trying to hide out in that room from you." Her head falls back on her shoulders as a short laugh escapes her. "We can see how well that turned out." Her gaze connects with mine again as her voice softens. "Not that I have a single regret over how things have turned out."

Relief floods my chest at her confession, easing the tension in my shoulders, my posture slouching a tad as I relax. "Good." I pop up on my elbows, leaning across the space between us to swipe a kiss against her lips, sealing our confessions away for now.

"What do you recommend?" I reach for the menu. "I'm fucking starving and could eat a damn horse."

"The eggs benedict are to die for here and my usual go-to, but since we missed breakfast, I'm a fan of their pizza. They make the brick oven kind here."

"I'm down with a pizza." I nod, browsing the menu. "Maybe a burger and fries too. Oh, and the buffalo cauliflower looks amazing too."

"That's a ton of food, Luc!" She chides on a giggle.

"I told you; I'm starving." I grin broadly back at her. "I can eat. Don't worry about that."

"Okay, if you say so." She shrugs, the smile never leaving her face as the waitress appears with our drinks and takes our order, leaving us to ourselves again.

I take a sip from the glass in front of me, the tart flavor of the salt and tomato bursting over my tongue. "Wow." I hum in approval. "These are good."

"Yep." She clinks her glass against mine, before tasting hers. "The best around."

I stare openly at her for a few minutes, watching her enjoy her drink as she looks out over the railing at the view before us.

"How old are you? Did I ask you that last night? I can't remember?"

One side of her mouth quirks up. "Don't you know it's not polite to ask a girl her age?"

"Just curious." I murmur as I pull another sip from my glass.

"I'm twenty-four." She provides without further prompting, her lips pursing a moment before she continues. "I don't think that breaks rule number one as long as I don't share my birthday with you."

I chuff out loud. "Okay, no birth dates allowed."

"Well?" She coaxes, red liquid sliding up the straw she has clamped between her lips as she sucks. Damn if that doesn't have my dick twitching.

"Well, what?" I respond, adjusting myself discreetly under the table.

"How old are you?" She inquires, eyes squirting in assessment as they peruse my face.

I forget she's not a rabid fan and doesn't really know anything about me. Different. In all the best ways. "I'm twenty-eight. Twenty-nine next month actually."

She holds up her hand. "Nope. I don't want to know when."

I shake my head, grinning. "It's not like you can't google it. I'm not a big fucking secret online."

"I won't though." She contends, her expression sincere, and it makes me fall just a little bit more for her.

"I believe you." It's weird getting to know someone organically. It's not a common thing in my world. There just isn't the opportunity for it.

I've almost forgotten what it's like to get to know someone in a normal way. Generally, everyone already knows everything about me, or at least, what they perceive is everything about me.

I'm wishing now that I didn't agree to rule number one so quickly because I realize I want to know more about this girl. And that in itself is a complete mindfuck. I'm leaving tomorrow. What good would getting to know anything more about her even do?

It's not like I'm going to have a relationship with someone after spending one day with them, let alone one where I'm on the road half the damn year. *Right?*

The food arrives and we share the pizza and fries, while I devour the burger and cauliflower. Conversation is easy while we eat. We keep it light and discuss arbitrary things like our favorite foods, the weather, and questions about my show that night.

I order another drink, but she switches to a diet coke, noting that she has to drive us back down a mountain. What I'd like to do is get a room here and hide away in it with her for the next twenty-four hours memorizing every inch of her body. Fuck the show tonight.

The thought stops my heart cold. I've never, not once in ten years, wanted to blow off a show. A sweat breaks out over my skin, goosebumps prickling in its wake.

Well, fuck.

This is new.

Haven't felt this before.

Is this what having a heart feels like?

Chapter Nine
Lily

I Was Made For Lovin' You
YUNGBLUD

"Would you let me drive her?"

We're standing outside the hotel entrance near valet, waiting for them to bring my car around when he asks.

"What about the drinks you had?"

He throws his head back as he laughs out loud. "Baby, I'm a rockstar. Two drinks are nothing. My tolerance is, well, let's just say that I'm completely sober right now."

"Well, you can't be completely sober." My forehead scrunching together as I watch him slide his glasses off, piercing me with a look that borders on haughty.

"Want to perform a sobriety test on me then, darling?"

He saunters a bit closer, grasping me around the waist before tugging me against his chest, a small gasp bursting from me when our bodies collide. "I assure you, I'm in *complete* control of all my facilities, but happy to demonstrate if you need."

My tongue darts out, wetting my bottom lip, our gazes locking, the best kind of tension sparking between us.

I arch a brow, tilting my head. "Can I trust you?"

"A little late for that question now, wouldn't you say?" His hand slides up to grip the back of my neck as he leans down, his lips feathering over mine as he speaks against them. "But I promise I'll take as good of care of your car as I have of you."

"You have been pretty nice to me so far." I concur, my body humming in remembrance at just *how* nice he'd been, but I wasn't quite ready to give in yet. "Do you have a driver's license?"

"You're fucking tough." He chuckles, pressing his forehead to mine, his fingers sliding into the hair at my nape. "Small but mighty you are, Kitten."

"I hate when you call me that." I pull my forehead from his and glance down.

"No you don't." He trails a finger down my cheek, using it to lift my chin until I'm looking into his eyes - *those damn whiskey eyes*. "You love that I have a nickname for you. And *that's* the part you hate."

"What?" I sputter, ready to argue, except the car is suddenly beside us, any words I had lost as the valet driver walks over to us.

"Here you go my man." Luc slides him a twenty before I even have a chance to catch up to the moment, and then strolls over to the driver's side of the car, flashing me a grin that only the devil himself could sport and not feel guilty.

"You better not crash my car." I point a finger, wagging it at him as the valet opens the passenger door for me.

I slide in, the door shutting behind me as I glare over at

my unexpected driver. He cocks his head toward my seat belt, sporting a smirk. "Better buckle up, baby."

"Luc, I'm serious." I wrench the belt over my chest as I shoot daggers at him.

"So am I."

He guns the engine and suddenly we're flying around the curve of the hotel exit and onto the mountain road, my body surging back into my seat before I can express another warning.

"Woo-hoo!" He hollers, a fist punching into the air through his open window. "This baby is smooth!"

The pure joy of his expression makes it impossible for me to be even a little bit angry at him.

"I don't think I've driven a car in over five months." He swings his gaze to me for a brief second, before looking back at the road. "This freedom feels fucking amazing."

He's cruising at a pretty high speed, but he has complete control of the vehicle, every corner we take, smooth and tight, my nerves, surprisingly calm. It's such a simple thing to let him drive, but one that obviously makes him utterly happy.

"Do you have a car at home?" I wonder out loud.

"A couple." He nods. "And a motorcycle, a Harley." He gives me another quick glance as he continues. "Our last break was from November until April, and I didn't do much driving then. Most of our time home was spent in the studio at my place, and if we did go somewhere, we were usually chauffeured."

"You have a studio in your house?" My brow shooting up as I'm reminded once again that I'm spending the day with an actual freaking rockstar.

"Yeah." He confirms. "When I had the place built, it was

the one thing I made sure I had. Makes it so much easier when we're not out on tour."

"Where do you live?" I'm genuinely curious to know where a rock god might choose to build a house.

"You sure this isn't breaking rule number one?" One side of his mouth quirking up.

"I'm not asking for your address, so I think we're good." I state matter-of-factly.

"I like how you get to modify the rules to your liking." He admonishes with a chuckle. "But I don't mind telling you, so it doesn't matter. I live just west of Chicago, in a suburb called Oak Park. It's where me and all the guys are from."

"I love that you still live in the town where you grew up. I would have thought you'd want to be in a big city."

"Nope." He shakes his head. "Like my town. Like being near my family. When I'm actually able to be home. Like that I'm left alone most of the time, cause most people know me from when I was just a little punk running around the village."

I'm about to ask about his family, but pause when he reaches for the volume on the radio and cranks it all the way up. "I love this song!" He shouts and then starts singing along, word for word, not missing a beat.

It takes a minute before I recognize the song, because it's not being sung by the original band, Kiss, and it's a little slower in tempo as well.

When the chorus comes on, Luc turns his head and stares at me as he sings, *"I was made for lovin' you, baby. You were made for lovin' me. And I can't get enough of you, baby. Can you get enough of me?"*

He looks and sounds so goddamn sexy that my heart does

several back flips as heat rushes to all the places in my body I'd like him to be touching. Right. Damn. Now.

"Pull the car over." I demand, not ask.

He swerves immediately to the side of the road, throwing the car in park, eyes wide as he turns to me. "What's wrong?"

I shake my head, my lower lip clenched between my teeth as I release my seat belt then surge in one motion to straddle him.

"Move the seat back." I order, my fingers shoving his hat off his head before tangling in his hair.

His brows shoot up, but he complies, the seat sliding back in one quick jerk, my center settling perfectly against his now hardening length, my mouth locking onto his. His hands grip around my waist, tighten, and yank me even tighter to his groin.

"We doing this right here?" He growls against my mouth as I rock my core against him.

"Right here." I nip his lower lip, then swipe my tongue over the bite. "Right now."

"And here I was thinking I was the bad one." His chest vibrates under me as he chuckles. His hands slide beneath my skirt and over my ass. "And this would have been so much easier if you had left these off."

I rise up on my knees and bring one leg over to the other. "Take them off." I breath out as I continue to ravage his mouth. My panties are off in less than three seconds, his jeans unbuttoned and shoved down to his thighs the next three seconds after that and a single after that, his cock plunges into me in one deep thrust.

"You're my new favorite feeling, baby." He groans, his head slamming back into the headrest, as I roll my hips back and forth. "Fucking hell."

"Right where the devil belongs." I pant, as I continue to slide up and down his shaft, every inch of me on fire as I ride him.

"Not going to last." He grunts, his eyes scrunching closed as his fingers dig into my skin so hard I know there will be bruises.

"Me either." I moan as I tighten and begin to convulse around the throbbing of his cock as he comes.

Stars.

So many stars.

And then heaven as my body becomes a feather and I float back to earth.

His arms slide around my back as he hugs me to his body, his chest rising and falling rapidly. "Where the hell did that come from?"

Before I can answer, a car passes, the horn beeping as it whizzes past us, laughter erupting from both of us as I scramble off his lap and back into the passenger seat. I open the glove compartment to grab some napkins, quickly wiping between my legs before I make a bigger mess.

Luc lifts his hips to tug his jeans up and over his waist, a wicked grin on his face. "I think I'll keep you on me for a little longer."

I feel my face flush, the reality of what we just did, *what I just did*, hitting home. I am not a girl who has sex in a car – let's not even mention it's my dead father's car – and certainly not on the side of the highway.

This guy seriously has me under some kind of spell and if I wasn't careful, I could quite possibly be needing to make a deal with the devil to get my sanity back after this.

"You okay?" Luc's fingers brush my hair back behind my ear before he tilts my head in his direction.

I nod, unable to find my voice, suddenly feeling shy and unsure about what I'm supposed to do next.

"Hey," He scoots over in his seat until he's able to cup my face with both his hands. "You didn't do anything wrong."

"I know." I murmur, nodding my head under his hold, my eyes darting to the floor.

"Look at me." His grip tightening by the smallest fraction, my gaze locking onto his. "What just happened was fucking amazing. Not wrong. Not dirty."

"I know." I repeat, but not with much conviction.

"I don't know what's going through your head, but let me be clear here; you are fucking perfect."

He kisses me. And it's soft and it's tender and also so perfect that I know walking away from him after today is going to be the hardest thing I've ever had to do.

Chapter Ten
Luc

Time In A Bottle
YUNGBLUD

I DRIVE us to the hotel because, number one, I have no idea how to get back to her place, and number two, I'm not ready to let her go yet. And, as much as I hate to admit it, I'm afraid if we go to her apartment, I'd be leaving there without her.

It's only a little after three so there's still plenty of afternoon left for us to spend together. And honestly, I wouldn't mind wasting that time up in my room, naked, but since I've already fucked her three times today, I don't want to push my luck.

"What do you feel like doing?" I drive into the valet lane, and hold my finger up to the valet so he knows I need a minute.

She shrugs, her damn lip clenched between her teeth again, and fuck if it doesn't make me want to suck it out and claim her mouth again. This girl is going to be my ruin, my goddamn downfall and she doesn't even have a clue.

"What can we do?" She glances out the window at the hotel entrance and then back at me. "I mean, people will know who you are if we're out in public, right?"

"Eh, sometimes." One side of my mouth tugs down. "Sometimes it's totally fine. The hat and glasses help a bit."

"Want to just walk around? It's actually not too hot out today." She suggests.

"Sure." I nod, thinking it's hot as fucking Hades, but want to do whatever she wants. "Let's give it a try. If things get ugly, I can call someone to grab us up."

I reach for the handle and open the door, the valet standing at the ready. He hands me a ticket, which I pass over to Lily, whose standing next to me now. She slides it into the little purse slung over her shoulder, and then I grab her hand and intwine my fingers with hers.

Her brow shoots up as she looks down to our joined hands and then back up at me, a smile lighting up her face, and that makes me smile right back at her. Yep, definitely going to be my ruin.

"Which direction?" I ask. "This is your town after all."

"Let's go this way." She turns to our left, tugging me with her. "I know a place that we might actually be able to hang out at and not be bothered this time of day."

"Cool." I slow my stride so I can match her smaller one, content to let someone else have control. "So, I'm not allowed to ask where you work, what your birthday is, or anything else too personal, so what do you want to talk about?"

"You." She tilts her head to look up at me. "Tell me about

the band, and what the guys are like, and what it's like when you're up on stage with everyone screaming your name."

"The guys are cool." I bob my head up and down as I think about how to explain how you can love and hate your best friends at the same time. "My brother is in the band, as you know, Mikey. He's the only one I want to murder most of the time. Dean, Mikey and I all grew up together; went to the same schools, started the band in high school. Dean met Hayden playing hockey. He's a couple years older than us, and probably the parent of the group."

I chuckle as I recall some of the crap we've been through and how many times Hayden has had to come bail our asses out of a jam. "They're all great guys. There's not much I wouldn't do for any one of them."

"That's really nice." She gives my hand a little squeeze. "Especially since you spend so much time together."

"Yeah, but don't get me wrong. As much as I love them, by the end of a tour, we're all ready to rip each other apart. Too much time together, too much booze, being in each other's spaces constantly wears thin."

"How much longer are on tour for?"

"One more month." I state. "And I'm ready for the break. We're not going to do another tour for at least a year. Just write and record. It's going to be amazing to just be in one place for a while."

"I can't even imagine what it's like living in hotel room after hotel room." She shakes her head, stopping at the intersection we've approached to wait until it's safe to cross. "The place is just another couple blocks up."

"It's cool. We have buses we stay on most of the time. We usually only stay in hotels when we're in a cool city like this." I scan the area around us, pleasantly relieved that no one seems to know who I am, or maybe they just don't care. "It's nice being able to walk around and not get mobbed."

The walk signal starts yapping that it's safe to proceed, so we move forward with the few other people that are waiting.

"Does that happen a lot to you? People just coming at you?" I can hear the concern in her voice, and it tugs at my heart, falling under her spell a little bit more.

"Depends where we are, honestly." I shrug. "It comes with the fame, and most people understand boundaries, but there's always the crazies. We usually have staff looking out for us, especially in situations when we're around large crowds." I let out a small chuff. "I've gotten some pretty fucked up shit in the mail, let me tell you."

"Oh, do tell me." She giggles. "I want to know."

"It's pretty nasty sometimes. Not going to lie. Dirty panties, naked pictures of girls, and guys too sometimes." I blow out a breath. "Got an actual wedding ring with a proposal letter once." I pause, frowning before I continue. "Probably the worst one was from a mother who sent me a letter blaming me for her kid's suicide. I guess one of my songs was on repeat in the room where she did it."

"Oh my God." She gasps and skids to a halt next to me. "That's horrible. How can someone blame you for something like that?"

She's so utterly beautiful as she stares at me. I cup her cheek gently with my free hand, swiping my thumb over her soft mouth. She has no idea how attractive her nativity about how shitty things can be in the world is to me.

"Because baby, she needed someone to blame. Someone to be angry at. I was that for her. And I just had to let that be okay. Even if it does haunt my fucking thoughts at least once a week."

"I'm so sorry you have to put up with that." She twists her head until her lips are against my palm, pressing a kiss to my skin. "It's not fair."

"It's the life I signed up for." I drop my hand and tug her forward. "Anyway, enough about that shit. Where's this place you're taking me to?"

"Right there." She points to a building that's set back a bit from the sidewalk, trimmed in a bright blue color, a big sign across the center of the roof, Peppermill. "It doesn't look like anything on the outside, but it's got a super chill vibe inside."

"I trust you." I assure her.

We're at the building in a matter of minutes, and I hold the door open for her as we both step inside. The cool air feels amazing after the heat outside.

It's essentially a really big diner, with lots of colorful booths and fake trees and greenery set up between the seating. There are a few people in the place, but not a single one even glances our way as we move further into the restaurant.

"Here." She pulls me to left. "This part is fine, but it's the lounge part that's cool."

I follow her into a darkened room, and stop beside her when she pauses. She looks over at me, I'm sure to gauge my reaction. She's right. It's pretty fucking cool.

There's a damn fireplace in a sunken pit in the center of the room, pink velour couches all around it. The lighting is a low, a dark pink or purple kind of glow. And the best part, it's practically empty. There's one other couple sitting at the bar, and that's it.

"Do you like it?" She asks, excitement bubbling in her tone.

"I like it." I flash her a grin. "You did good."

"Come on." She tugs me toward the bar. "Let's get a drink and then we can go sit at the fireplace."

We do just that. We each order a beer. I throw some cash up on the bar, and we get cozy on one of the couches. She curls her knees up against her side, and leans into me, my arm slung casually around her. She fits like she was made for me.

"This is nice." I take a sip of my beer, staring into the flames flickering in soft waves, contemplating the simple enjoyment of being able to do something like this. It hasn't happened in a long time. I'm not sure what kind of juju is allowing this in my universe right now, but I'm not even going to question it. There's no way I want to jinx this.

"It is." She agrees, snuggling into me a little more. "What time do you have to get ready for your show?"

"We've got time." I tighten my grasp on her shoulder to keep her close. "You're going to come tonight, right?" I feel her body tense under my hold, my pulse increasing as a result. "What's wrong?"

"Well, um, I don't have a ticket. I only went last night because Bri had them and needed someone to go with her." She stammers out in a rush.

Relief floods through me, a soft chuckle rumbling through my chest at how easily I can solve what she thinks is a problem. "I think I can take care of that."

"Are you sure?" She sits up straight and turns to look at me. "I don't want to take advantage of you."

This fucking girl. She has no idea how adorable she is. I flash her a wicked grin as I shake my head. "Unlike what you did to me in your car?"

Her cheeks flame a dark pink, her bottom lip instantly

sucked between those teeth again. Jesus, why does that make my dick so fucking hard?

"That was your fault." She blusters, sticking her chin out in defiance.

I chuff loudly in protest. "How was that my fault?"

She rests back on her calves, takes a sip of her beer, maybe for courage, and dives into her defense. "If you hadn't looked so damn hot singing, telling me you were made for loving me, looking all sexy, I wouldn't have done, you know, what I did."

I throw my head back as laughter bellows out of me. When I find her eyes again, her brow is furrowed like she can't believe my reaction.

"Kitten, I'll sing to you every damn hour of the day if that's the reaction I'm going to get." I lean forward, closing the gap between us to crush my mouth to hers. She melts into me, my arm wrapping around her back to pull her closer.

She pushes away a minute later, her eyes peering up at me under her lashes, her body still flush to mine. "You have to stop."

I cock my head, confused. "Why?"

She huffs out a heavy sigh. "You're a rock star, and you'll be gone in a day, and you have this huge life, and because, even though I don't want to, I'm starting to like you."

Her voice lowers to almost a whisper as she continues to stare at me. "I wish we never met because you're going to be so hard to forget. Being with you is like playing with fire."

"Then burn with me." I growl back, kissing her hard, not willing to listen to any of the sense I know she's making, because fuck me, I don't think I'm going to be able to let her go anyway.

Chapter Eleven
Lily

Sparks Fly
Taylor Swift

WE STAY at the Peppermill another hour, kissing, drinking beers, kissing, sharing things that aren't of any real relevance, and more amazing kissing. The man has lips that were made for dangerous things.

We tear ourselves away from each other long enough to walk back to the hotel. We don't say much. But things feel heavy, loaded, my hand encased possessively in his the entire time, meaning more than it probably should.

And I don't think it's in my head. This *thing* that seems to be developing so very quickly between us. It's scary as hell. We're both seem to plunging ahead anyway, unsure where the chips may fall, ignoring the fact he's leaving tomorrow.

But it is only a month until his tour is over. He said he'd be in one place for at least the next year after that. So, maybe? Maybe this is something that could actually happen.

I can't even believe I'm even entertaining the idea of this, of him. Especially given how gross I thought it was that Bri wanted to hook up with Dean. And now, look at me.

Shit. I still need to get the damn Plan B pill before it's too late. I cringe internally, not ideal, but damn, worth it.

"You're awfully quiet over there." His hand gently squeezes mine as he glances my way. "You good?"

"Yup." I nod. "Was wondering if I should go home and change?" My lie coming out smooth as glass.

His eyes scan my body from head to toe, one corner of his mouth kicking up in a crooked smile. "Please don't."

"Really?" My heart thumping wildly under my ribs from the scorching look he just delivered. "I feel like this might be a little too frilly for your crowd."

"I don't give a fuck what anyone else thinks." His tone low and possessive. "I love what you're wearing and think you look amazing. Just the way you are."

"Okay." I purse my lips between my teeth, trying to hold back the smile threatening to break free.

"You know I'm not leaving tomorrow without your number and address, right?" He tosses the demand out like he's asking if the sky is blue, my head spinning off into the clouds now that I know for sure we're on the same page.

When I don't answer after a second, he skids to a halt, yanking me to a stop next to him. "I don't want to hear another fucking word about rule number one. This-" He wags a finger back and forth between us. "This isn't up for debate. I will be seeing you again. One way or another."

His gaze bores into me, people brushing past us as we stand frozen in the middle of the sidewalk, inside our very own bubble.

He leans in, voice low. "I don't lose what I want." He cocks his head as he waits for me to respond.

"Okay." I squeak out, my breath caught in my lungs as my pulse swooshes through my veins.

"That sounds like maybe you aren't sure?" He takes a possessive step closer to me. "If that's not what you want, tell me now, cause shit, I'm already counting the days until I'm off this damn tour and able to see you again."

I'm reeling. His words make me weak in the knees and the world feels like it's spinning as I try and regain my balance. How is this even happening right now?

"Yes." I nod emphatically, then throw my arms around his neck as I surge against him, whispering my consent in his ear. "It's definitely what I want."

He wraps me in an embrace so tight I gasp, but not in pain, in pure joy. He holds me for a solid minute before slowly releasing me, settling my feet back on earth, his forehead pressing to mine. "Did the angel just make a deal with the devil?"

"Don't make me regret it." I plead, truly fearful of what he may do to my heart.

He brushes a kiss across my lips as he shakes his head before stepping back. "I promise."

<hr>

THE NEXT FIVE hours are a complete whirlwind. When we arrive back at the hotel, Luc is bombarded by his manager, then his band mates for not showing up for soundcheck, (oops), and finally his costume people, who drag him away to get dressed for the show.

There are other people in the room, and I feel awkward and out of place. I don't know a single person, and no one is going out of their way to introduce themselves or make me feel especially welcome. But, I'm guessing having random women hanging out isn't anything new to them. And most are probably extremely temporary, so why bother making the effort.

When Luc finally appears again, it's about a half-hour before the band has to go on. I can sense he's feeling rushed as he scrapes a hand through his hair, downs two beers in less than ten minutes, all while pacing back and forth.

I'm leaning against a wall near the bar when he stalks toward me, his hands coming up to rest on either side of my head as he leans into me. "Hey."

"Hey." I reply, blinking up at him.

"You okay?" He takes a step closer, his lower half meeting mine, the heat of him radiating against my bare legs.

"Uh-huh." I murmur, wishing I was anywhere but here with him. I loop a finger around the chain hanging on his neck and tug it down until his lips meet mine. "How long is this show?" I ask as his lips move against mine.

He chuckles, a wicked smirk displaying as he tilts his head back a fraction. "Too fucking long."

He presses another kiss to my mouth, then steps back, grabbing my hand. "We're going down." With his other hand, he tugs the hood up of the sweatshirt he has on, over his head, hiding most of his face.

He breaks into a stride, his fingers holding mine tight, and leads me behind the entourage leaving the room. "We play for just a little under two hours. You can watch from the side of the stage. I'll show you when we get down there."

We step onto an elevator, and he tugs me up against his body, wrapping an arm around me protectively.

"See that dude right there." He nods his head at a man to

our left. "That's Jake." His voice raises as he yells over to him. "Hey Jake, say hi to Lily."

Jake gives a little salute and nods his head in greeting. Luc continues addressing him. "Make sure you give her anything she needs and look out for her. Got it?"

"You got it, Boss." Jake nods again. I make sure to memorize what he looks like and what he's wearing so I can find him if I need him.

The elevator comes to a stop, the doors sliding open, our entourage spilling out into a hallway. Luc keeps a firm hold on me, making me feel protected and safe, but I'm still nervous about what I should do when he's up on the stage.

It's a completely different perspective going to a concert *with* the band, instead of *for* the band. Bri is going to absolutely kill me when I tell her about all of this. Probably with her bare hands. I giggle at the thought, and the irony of this entire situation.

"What's so funny?" Luc glances my way.

"I was just thinking about Bri." I let out another little burst of laughter. "My friend from last night. She's the one who is completely obsessed with your band. She's going to be so mad when she finds out I got to see the show from backstage."

"Wait til you tell her you also bagged the lead singer." He smirks wickedly.

I slide a hand down my face as I shake my head. "She won't believe it. Probably not in a million years."

He tugs me over to the side of the hallway and comes to a stop. "Get your phone out." He points to my purse.

I do as he says, and slide it out.

"Unlock it." He requests, and when I do, takes it from me. He drapes one arm over my shoulder, presses my cheek against his through the hoodie, and then angles the phone to take a selfie. He hands the phone back to me with a nod. "Now you have proof."

Before I can even react, he's got my hand in his again and begins striding to catch up with the rest of the band. As we continue down the hall, the music from the opening band begins to grow louder, so I know we must be close to our destination.

Sure enough, moments later, we're in a side room off of the stage area that's littered with couches, tables filled with every snack you could imagine, and a large open cooler filled with ice and a variety of beverage choices.

"Do you want anything?" Luc asks, snagging a beer for himself, twisting the top off.

"I'll have a beer." He hands the open bottle to me, and then grabs another for himself, slugging down a few swallows.

"We gotta get mic'd up." He nods toward the other guys in the band, already getting taking care of by some of the crew. "Once we go on, you can stand anywhere you want on the side of the stage. If you need anything, anything at all, just find Jake."

"Okay." I nod as he kisses me quickly, then strolls a few feet away. I watch as he tugs the hoodie completely off before a tech clips a wireless pack to his belt and runs a cord under his shirt. He pops a bud into each ear, and then rolls his shoulders, like he's stretching before a workout.

He's back in front of me a few blinks later, snagging my hand again as he leads me out of the room and toward the stage. My heart is thundering in my chest, and I can't help but wonder what this feels like for him. Going up on stage in front of thousands of people screaming for him, for them.

"Okay." He has to yell in order for me to hear him. "I'll see you on the other side." His hand wraps around the back of my head as he drags me in for a kiss that takes my breath away, and then he's gone.

I stare as he walks onto the stage, the crowd roaring the moment they see him, and I watch in awe as he comes alive. He owns that stage, the fans, guitar and drums exploding into life as he begins to sing.

As I bear witness to it all, I wonder how in the hell I ever could have thought anything other than how completely and utterly incredible he is.

Chapter Twelve
Luc

Angels Like You
Miley Cyrus

I SLIP IN MY IN-EARS, the world dulling instantly until all I can hear is the low thrum of my own pulse. One twist of the dial and the stage roars to life in my head—the crowd, the hum of amps, the bass warming up.

I roll my shoulders, stretching out the last of the tension. Strapped in, synced, untethered. No leash. No limits. Only sound. And I'm about to drown them all in it.

I love this part of the fucking show. The anticipation. The roar of the crowd when I step onto the stage. It's what fuels me and keeps me going every night.

I sneak a glance at Lily. She's got her lip clamped in her damn teeth again, and while I think it's fucking adorable, I've come to realize it's what she does when she's nervous. I want her to feel welcome, at ease here behind the stage with me.

As soon as Kirk is finished wiring me up, I go to her.

She's like a magnet I can't seem to ignore the pull of. And one that surprisingly, I don't want to. I remind myself again, this is not the time to fall for anyone, ignoring my own advice as I snag her hand in mine.

I stop, kissing Lily with all I've got so she knows that no matter what happens out on that stage, it's her I'm thinking of and can't wait to get back to.

The house lights drop and the world detonates. A roar rises from the dark like a living, breathing beast, thousands of voices fusing into one relentless scream that rattles my chest harder than the bass ever could.

I step out into it, into them, and the spotlight slams into me. Heat, blinding and white, washes over my skin, but it's nothing compared to the fire burning inside. My pulse thrums in sync with the pounding drums behind me, a heartbeat amplified until it feels like I own every vein in the room.

Hands shoot up. Cell phone lights flicker like stars scattered across a velvet sky. For a split second, the crowd is mine. Mine to command, mine to break, mine to lift higher than they've ever been.

I wrap my fingers around the mic, the metal warm from the heat of the stage, and I grin like the devil they came here to see.

Then I open my mouth. The first line tears out of me raw and sharp, slicing straight through the roar, and the place *erupts*. The sound of my own voice, amplified, fed back into me with their screams. It's pure gasoline. Every note I spit is fire, every lyric a spark, and they burn for me, howl for me, beg for more.

I always thought that this—*this*—is the closest thing to heaven I'd ever get, but as I turn my head, find Lily, and flash her a grin, I know I may have found something even better. She's the calm in a storm I didn't even know I was caught in.

Her cheeks are lifted in the biggest grin, her body bopping to the beat, her arms raised in the air. Witnessing her jamming out to my music is a fucking high that surges a burst of energy into my performance. Every growl, every thrust of my hips, every song I sing tonight, it's for her.

I love the fucking stage, but as we belt out our final song, I can't wait to get back to her. I bow with the band, wave to the crowd and have to restrain myself from running in her direction as we leave the stage.

When I reach her, I wrap her in a hug, swooping her off her feet, swinging her in a circle, hoping she doesn't mind I'm drenched in sweat. Doesn't seem to be an issue as her arms loop around my shoulders to press herself tighter to me.

"You were-" She begins before I seal my lips over hers, stealing the breath from her. Her chest vibrates as laughter bubbles and she breaks our kiss, her eyes meeting mine. "Luc, seriously, you were amazing."

I flash a wicked grin as I slide her down my body, onto her feet. "I told you."

She swats me lightly on the arm. "Cocky much?"

"Nope." I arch a single brow. "Don't need to be." I tilt my head toward the stage where members of the crowd are calling for another encore. "Listen to that."

"It's surreal." She shakes her head, her hand lifting over her mouth as she stares out past the stage. "I can't believe this is your life."

"Not my life." I nod in thanks when Jake walks by and hands me a towel. I use it to scrape the sweat from hair, face and neck, then wrap it around my shoulders. "It's my job."

"Pretty sweet job." She muses, staring wide-eyed at the small crowd gathered backstage as our crew work on each one of us to strip us of our wiring.

"Not complaining one bit." I flash her a quick smile, thank Jake as he hands me my phone, and then direct my focus back to her. "Ready to get out of here?"

"Is there another party tonight?" Her sneakered foot scuffs back and forth as she peers up at me. It was pretty clear what she witnessed last night was not her scene. And although she didn't know it, I was so over it as well.

"There's always another party." I admit, noticing the slump in her shoulders almost immediately in response. "But I've got other plans for us."

Her posture straightens, a small smile gracing her features. "Really? You don't have to go?"

"Nope." I drape my arm over her shoulders and lead her down the hallway we came from earlier. "I had Jake get me my own room." I glance down to gauge her reaction, satisfaction washing over me when I witness the evident expression of relief on her face. "You cool just hanging with me."

Her hair swishes against my arm as she nods her head. "Totally cool with that."

"Sweet." I already had Jake move all my shit earlier, not wanting to chance having to go to the suite and then getting pressured into staying. Jake had also already transferred the room key to my phone, making us getting up there a piece of cake.

We step onto the elevator and I press the button for the 23rd floor. Not quite the penthouse, but I told Jake to get me a room to impress, so I'm sure it'll be nice. I have to swipe my key to get up to the floor, so I slide my phone out of my pocket and find it in the wallet app and scan it before the elevator finally starts to rise.

As we're climbing, I notice all Lily has with her is a purse. Didn't exactly know how the day, let alone this night, was going to pan out and realize my planning really isn't doing shit for her.

"Anything you need I can arrange for you." I tug her flush to my body and gleam wickedly at her. "Except clothes. I'd really prefer you naked for the next twelve hours."

Her lips purse as she peers up at me, her eyes narrowing as she scans my face. When she speaks, her words are laced with sarcasm. "Oh, you thought I'd be spending the night again?"

"You bet your fucking sweet ass I do." I palm her cheek, tilting her head back so that her mouth is more accessible. I lean in and trace over her lips with my tongue, plunging inside when her mouth opens on a gasp. I release her face to lift both her arms, locking them above her as I use my body to push her back against the mirrored wall of the elevator.

Her leg hooks higher around my thigh, pulling me closer, and I grind into her, the heat of her body scorching through the denim of my jeans. My mouth devours hers until the elevator dings, doors sliding open on another floor. She stiffens, but I don't let her go. I kiss her harder, daring her to pull away, daring her to remember we're not alone yet.

No one steps inside though. The doors close again, and I chuckle darkly against her lips. "Careful, Kitten. Elevators have cameras."

I nip her jaw, tongue tracing down her throat as she arches, desperate for more. I keep her pinned, giving her just enough friction to wreck her, but not enough to satisfy.

"Patience," I growl in her ear, pressing harder as the

elevator climbs. "I promise to ruin you properly the second that door closes upstairs."

When it finally dings on our floor, I don't waste time. My hand clamps around her wrist, dragging her down the plush hallway. She laughs breathlessly, her tiny feet shuffling to keep up, but she doesn't try to stop me. I flash my phone key over the scan, the lock clicks, and I shove the door open.

The second it shuts behind us, I press her against it, not to take, but to tease. My mouth hovers a hair's breadth from hers, my thumb stroking her bottom lip as she pants against me. I could kiss her, devour her again, but I want the ache to build, so I can unravel her by inches. I want this time to last between us.

I skim my hand down her arm, over the curve of her hip, and stop just short of where she wants me most. Her eyes flash with need, and I grin wickedly.

"Bedroom," I rasp. "Now. Unless you want me to fuck you against this door where the whole goddamn hallway can hear."

Her eyes spark with fire at my threat, but instead of arguing, she slips out from under me, chin tipped high. She saunters toward the bedroom like she owns the place, hips swaying, knowing damn well I'm watching every step.

"You don't scare me Luc." She throws over her shoulder, her tone light but laced with challenge.

"You should be, Lily." I warn, my voice low, rough, the sound echoing through the suite as I follow. I don't hurry. I want her to feel my presence stalking behind her, every step deliberate, the air between us sparking with electric current.

She reaches the doorway to the bedroom and pauses, fingers skimming the doorframe. I crowd in behind her, pressing my chest to her back, my lips brushing her ear. "This is your last chance to change your mind."

Her answering laugh is soft, daring. "You afraid of what might happen if I stay?"

I drag my knuckles down her arm, slow and teasing, before capturing her wrist, guiding her across the threshold. The lights glow soft and golden against the crisp sheets and sprawling king bed. I spin her to face me, pinning her with a look that leaves no room for doubt.

"Not even a little bit." I rasp, lifting her chin so her gaze locks on mine. "I know exactly what's going to happen. And I plan on taking my time making it happen. I'm going to explore every single inch of you tonight, and I won't be stopping until you've screamed my name multiple times."

She blinks, her eyes wide, but not a single ounce of fear reflects back at me. "You're dangerous."

A laugh bellows out of me, my head falling back on my shoulders for a second before I lower my chin, a feral grin breaking across my cheeks. "Now who's afraid?"

"Not afraid." She refutes. "Just stating the facts." Her button nose scrunching up as her gaze travels down my sweaty frame. "How about a shower first?"

"Just going to get dirty again." I promise on a growl as I swipe a kiss across her mouth, anxious to have her underneath me again. "Not sure what the point is."

"The point is that you stink." Laughter tumbles from her, making it harder to alter my focus anywhere but her lips. I do though. I take a step back on a sigh, hating that she's right.

"Okay, but only if you join me." I turn, crooking a finger for her to follow, peeling off the shirt that's plastered to my skin, dropping it in our wake.

Her gaze raking down my body has my cock throbbing

against the zipper of my pants. I want inside her right fucking now, but I also want to savor every moment of her. Whether or not I want to admit it out loud, I know that what's happening between us is something different.

I stop next to the shower, turn it on, then bend to tug my boots off. While I'm still kneeling, I unlace her chucks and slowly pull them off her feet, one shoe at a time. I slide each bobby sock off, revealing perfect, feminine feet, the tips of her toes painted a pale pink.

I press a kiss against the top of her knee as I rise, my fingers going to the ties at the top of her shoulders next. I tug one and then the other undone, the dress sliding down her body in a single swoosh of fabric.

She's left in a simple white cotton strapless bra and matching panties, and damn if it's not the sexiest thing I've ever seen on a girl.

"You're a fucking shining star on a moonless night." I observe in awe at the simplicity of her, and how it only makes her so much more.

"Luc." She whispers, fingers skimming down my chest until they find the button on my pants, popping them open. "Don't fall for me."

"Might be a bit too late for that." Surprising myself with the confession. I shove my pants down my legs, and pull them off. When I'm naked in front of her, I tug her against me, her mouth falling open in a small huff of shock when our bodies connect. "We'll figure this out. I'm only on tour for another month."

Her blue topaz irises stare back at me, her brow free of any worry for once. Her silence has me doubting if she wants the same thing, so I just ask the question. "If that's what you want."

Her head slowly begins to nod up and down, her lips curving up to form a smile. "It is."

"Good." I let out a breath I didn't realize I had trapped in my lungs.

"Now that that's settled, let's get in the damn shower so I can keep my earlier promise." I slap her lightly on the ass when she shimmies her undies off, and have her naked under the falling water before she can utter another word.

SUNLIGHT CREEPS across the hotel curtains, slicing through the haze of sleep. My arm reaches for her automatically, like my body already knows where she should be; warm, soft, and tucked against me.

But the sheets are cold. Empty.

I blink, push up on one elbow. The purse that sat on the chair is gone. The dress I untied, one bow at a time at her shoulders is no longer lying on the bathroom floor. The adorable chucks I unlaced last night are nowhere to be found.

My chest tightens, heat pricking the back of my neck. Maybe she's out in the living area?

I get up, not caring I'm nude, and stride through the rest of the suite. It's empty. I check the bathroom. Not even a trace of steam or water in the sink to indicate she showered or washed up.

Maybe she went downstairs to grab coffee? She knows she could have ordered anything she wanted off the room service menu. But I also know how independent she is, and can imagine her going down to grab something in the lobby to save me money.

My eyes roll at the very thought, the tiniest bit of relief hitting me at this logic.

Twenty minutes later, she still isn't back though. And the longer I sit in silence, the louder the panic grows.

We had figured this out. We agreed. We both said it's what we wanted. That we would find a way.

Those words actually kept me awake last night long after she fell asleep in my arms. I'd already started picturing her beside me, and not just for one night, but for all the nights.

I shove off the bed, pace the room, check the hallway. Nothing. No note. No trace. It's like she was never here at all.

A hollow ache cracks my ribs wide open. I shouldn't feel like this. Thirty-six hours isn't enough to break a man, but fuck if I don't feel shattered.

I press the heels of my hands into my eyes, but the image of her looking at me, like I was more than just a rockstar, more than a sin to taste and forget, burns into the darkness.

Where the fuck is she?

I stumble back into the room, rage starting to drown out my worry. Anger is easier. Anger I can live with.

If she thinks she can walk away from me, from us and what we could be, she's wrong.

Did she use me? No. I know what happened was real for both of us.

I dig through my clothes scattered across the floor until I find my phone, but as I swipe the screen to open it, I realize we never even exchanged numbers.

I never even asked what her last name was. I couldn't even try to find her on social. And the only picture we took was the one I snapped of us last night right before the show. And that was on *her* phone, not mine.

And yeah, we went to her apartment, but *she* had ordered

the Uber we took yesterday, and there was no way in hell I was ever going to be able to remember how the hell to get back to her place.

I lift my phone to find the contact information for Dean and call him. It takes about six rings before he answers, his voice groggy. "What the fuck, dude. It's eight in the damn morning."

"Did you get the number off that girl you hooked up with the other night?" I demand, thinking this may be my way back in to Lily.

"Gonna need to be a little more specific than that my friend. Which night and which girl?" A grumbling chuckle follows his question.

"Night before last." I think trying to remember what day today is. It was easy with our maddening schedule to forget what day it was, let alone what city we are in.

"Wednesday night." I state with wary confidence; pretty sure today is Friday.

A long sigh is all I hear, straining my already broken patience, before he finally responds. "What did she look like, do you remember?"

"I don't know, man." I scrape a hand through my hair as I pace the floor trying to recall her friend. "She was a brunette. Longish hair. She did tequila at the bar with that blonde friend of hers, in the little red skirt."

My mind rewinds to that moment I first saw her, a bolt of pain stabbing through my chest at the thought of not seeing her again.

"Oh yeah." He hums through the phone, satisfaction lacing the action. "Briana. Firecracker that one was."

"Did you get her number?" I pray to God above that he did, even though in my gut, I know the prospect of it is pretty fucking low.

A hard grunt. "Fuck no. You know it ain't like that for me. One and done."

"Fuck!" I bark out before hanging up on him. No point in continuing that conversation.

I'll find her. I don't care how long it takes.

I'll burn down the fucking world if I have to. Start with the clubs, end with the city. Whatever it takes.

Chapter 13
Luc

Dead Inside
Blackbear

Michelle Windsor

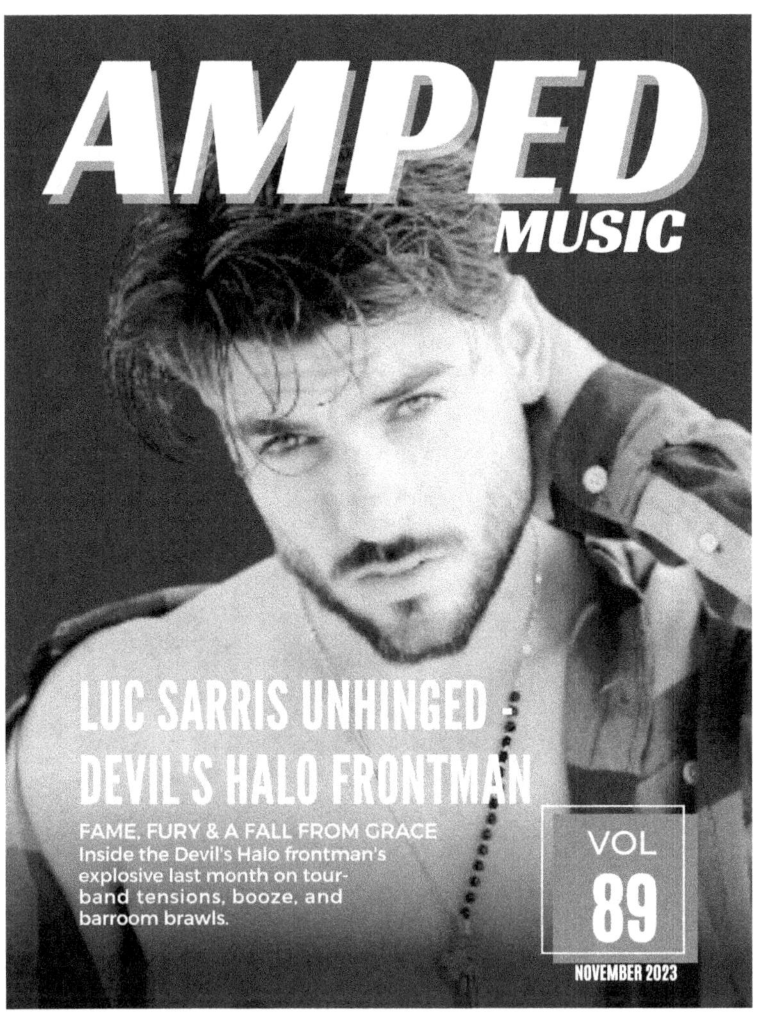
AMPED
MUSIC
LUC SARRIS UNHINGED -
DEVIL'S HALO FRONTMAN
FAME, FURY & A FALL FROM GRACE
Inside the Devil's Halo frontman's
explosive last month on tour-
band tensions, booze, and
barroom brawls.
VOL
89
NOVEMBER 2023

Weekly

UNPLUGGED

NOVEMBER 5, 2023

Your Backstage Pass to Chaos.

MGK'S WEDDING
FIRST LOOK

DEVIL'S HALO:
HELL HATH
NO FURY LIKE
A SINGER
SCORNED

LATEST TOUR
NEWS & DATES

Visit our website
WWW.UNPLUGGEDWKLY.COM

Chapter 14
Luc

We Are The Champions
QUEEN

AMPED
MUSIC
FROM CHAOS TO CROWN
DEVIL'S HALO REIGNS SUPREME
ASHES & ECHOES
This isn't just a comeback album—
it's a confession set to a riff. Luc
Sarris and his band deliver the
album of the decade.
VOL
51
JULY 2024

Weekly

UNPLUGGED

NOVEMBER 2024

Your Backstage Pass to Chaos.

FULL LIST OF
GRAMMY NOMS

DEVIL'S HALO:
STRIKES
GOLD, PLATINUM
AND
5 GRAMMY NOMS

REMEMBERING
LIAM PAYNE

WWW.UNPLUGGEDWKLY.COM

February 2025
GRAMMY
EDITION
MUSIC
DAILY
Full list of
this year's
award
winners
The big
Taylor Swift
snub
All about
Beyonce's
performance
Devil's Halo's Redemption
Four awards -including
Album of the Year.
Full interview with
Luc Sarris inside.

Chapter 15
Luc

The Night We Met
Lord Huron

"I can't believe we're back in this damn city, man." I pace in front of the large plate-glass window that overlooks the lights of the Vegas strip. My arms are crossed over my chest, where beneath, my heart is beating irrationally hard.

"We had to, Luc." Dean takes a swig of the beer he's holding, his posture comfortably sprawled on one of the four couches in the massive living room. His gaze tracks my movement, bouncing back and forth like he's watching a tennis match. "You know it's always a huge turn-out here." He shakes his head. "And it's the fucking Sphere, man."

"I know, I know." I sigh, throwing a glance his way. "I didn't think it was going to be this tough."

"Dude, it's been almost two years." Dean scratches his chin, one side of his mouth tugging down. "None of us thought-" He shrugs before finishing his sentence. "Well, none of us thought it would be an issue. I mean, it's been almost two years, and you only spent two nights with that damn chick."

My body stiffens as I come to an abrupt halt, turning to look at Dean. He's my best friend. We've been through everything you can possibly imagine two guys going through, and I do mean everything. But fuck me if I don't want to punch him in the damn face right now. He knows better than anyone what two nights with "that chick" did to me.

"Lily." I growl out. "Her name is Lily, and you know damn fucking well she wasn't just some *damn chick* to me."

"Sorry." He throws his hands above his head in surrender, standing as he does. "Shouldn't have said that."

He strides over to me, clapping a hand on my shoulder, his next words coming out gentle. "You have to let her go, Luc. If she wanted to see you, find you, she would have."

I know he's right. It's been one year, nine months, and four days since we were together. Not that I'm counting. I clap him back on the shoulder, nodding, instead of providing a verbal response, and begin pacing again.

He strolls behind the bar and grabs another beer from the large glass fridge. "Hey, at least they agreed to book us in a different hotel this time. That has to help a little bit, right?" He twists the top off the bottle as he asks the question.

"Sure." I acquiesce, not really believing that anywhere within a hundred miles of this place is going to do anything but remind me of her.

It's only two o'clock. I don't have to prep for the show for another five hours. I'm going to wear a hole through this carpet if I stay here.

"I'm gonna go take a walk." I decide out loud. I head for

the stairs that lead up to my room so I can grab a hat and some glasses.

"You want company?" Dean asks as I pass him.

"Nah." I throw over my shoulder. "Will make it more obvious if we're together."

"You going to be okay?" Concern in his tone as I start trotting up the stairs.

I understand why he's worried. I do. I was a train wreck for six weeks after we left Vegas the last time we were here. Fucked so much shit up for us. And while I'm definitely feeling things I thought I'd put behind me, I'm tight. I'm not going to spiral again.

"I'm good, man." I assure him. "I'll find you if things get heavy."

Fifteen minutes later I step off the elevator into a hallway that leads through the casino. It's the only way out, unless I wanted to go through the hassle of finding one of my security guards and having them lead me through a maze of back hallways to a staff elevator.

The thing about Vegas, especially in the casino, most people are focused on the machine in front of them, and don't even notice what's happening around them.

Being recognized has only gotten worse over the last year. Especially with all the attention we received over album of the year. Kind of ironic. It was this town, *that damn chick*, as Dean likes to refers to Lily, that inspired every song on our album, Ashes & Echoes.

I guess something good came out of it. If I wanted to try and keep things positive, that's probably the only way I was going to get through being in this city again.

I maneuver through the casino, relief surging through me when I see the doors to freedom just a short stroll away. I take a second to scan the large expanse of the lobby, noticing a few people standing in line to check-in. My gaze travels to the staff behind the large counter, and I almost trip as I skid to a stop, my breath freezing in my lungs.

I tear the sunglasses off my face, blinking several times to assure myself that what I'm seeing is real and not a mirage. But no. It's real. I gawk for a full minute, absorbing every motion she makes as she assists an attendant checking in what appears to be a difficult guest.

Her smile, her eyes the color of ice, the sprinkle of freckles across her nose. Exactly the same. The only thing different is her hair. It's not as long, only falling a little past her shoulders now, but still the golden blonde color I remember.

I close my mouth, realizing its hanging wide, and slide my sunglasses back on. I inch my way over to an arm chair that's in the lobby, but far enough away that she might not see me. I collapse into it, my chest rising and falling in such a way that I realize I'm panting. I haven't taken my eyes off her, afraid she'll disappear again if I do. What the hell am I supposed to do now?

I swore I wouldn't look for her. That I had forgotten the taste of her. The way she had looked at me like I was worth saving. But one look at her across the lobby, and suddenly every lie I told myself falls apart in my hands. She ruined me, yet, here I am, craving more destruction from her.

We deliberately chose a different hotel to stay at. The guys did everything in their power to try and make sure this wouldn't happen. The last thing they wanted was for me to spiral again. Obviously someone, or something, in the damn universe has a strange fucking sense of humor.

She works here. Out of all the hotels in Las Vegas, she works *here*. Irony at its damn best.

Her head lifts, and I duck mine, looking down at the floor like it's the most interesting thing I've ever seen. What if she sees me? I have no idea what she would do. Would she pretend she didn't? Pretend we didn't have the two most amazing nights of my life together?

I blow out an unsteady breath, and tilt my head just enough to be able to peek up under the brim of my hat. She doesn't seem to have noticed me, her attention back on the guest in front of her. My heart is racing, galloping like it's on the last turn at the Kentucky Derby.

Do I go up and say something to her? What if she gets pissed? What if she acts like she doesn't remember me? What if she makes a scene? That's all I fucking need. But what if I can finally get an answer to why the hell she ghosted me?

I hear clicking on the marble tile a few feet away from me. I shift my gaze toward the sound, my stomach bottoming out when I realize it's her. All rational thought leaves my brain as I push myself up and mindlessly close the space between, forcing her to either maneuver around me or stop.

She stops. Abruptly. Her hand landing on my forearm to keep herself from bouncing into me, sparks of lightening singeing over my skin from her touch.

"I'm so sorry." Her touch gone a second later as she peers up at me. "I didn't see you coming."

Everything around me stills. The dinging of slot machines, people chattering, the music playing overhead, the wheeling of suitcases. All I hear is her. And it's like a thousand angels singing the most beautiful chorus. All I can do is stare at her. It's really fucking her.

"Are you okay?" Her head tilts, and again, her skin is on mine as she rests a hand against my arm in concern. I can't help it. I check to see if she's wearing a ring, relief washing over me that she isn't.

"Lily?" I finally breathe out, finding my voice.

Her touch is gone again, her arms crossing over her chest as she regards me. "I'm sorry, have we met?"

My brow furrows. I lift a hand and use a finger to slide my glasses down my nose and off my face. I wait to see if anything registers, but her face remains blank.

"You're kidding, right?" I can't help the venom my voice is laced with.

Now it's her brow that furrows, her head cocking slightly as her gaze locks onto mine. "Your eyes..." Her lower lip slides between her teeth, and that single action almost has a guttural moan leaving me.

"Whiskey eyes." I remind her. "That's how you described them to me."

"So, we know each other?" Her brow furrows deeper, genuine curiosity in her question.

"Are you seriously going to play this fucking game with me?" I take a step back, shaking my head. "It's bad enough you ghosted me, but to pretend you don't remember me?"

My hand grips my throat, dragging down its length roughly. Better mine than hers right now. "Un-fucking-believable."

"When?" She completely ignores the fact that I'm getting angry, and instead, steps closer to me, a look of urgency expressed in her features. "When did we know each other?"

Is she for real right now? I glance around, and notice there's a small crowd starting to gather around us. *Great, just fucking great. The cherry on the top of the fucking sundae.*

"Look, can we do this somewhere else?" I tilt my head toward the small hoard. "This is about to get ugly."

She considers the group of gawkers behind us, then nods. "Follow me."

Without hesitation, she turns on her heel and leads me to a door behind the mammoth check-in counter. She doesn't stop walking as we enter a hallway. She continues until she reaches a door on the left, her name, "Lilith Anderson", on the front. I finally, *finally* know her full name.

She swipes a badge over the sensor above the knob, then pushes the door open, holding it for me to enter. Once I'm through, she strides past me, the door slamming in her wake. The office isn't anything special. A 10x10 room with a desk centered on the far side wall, facing out, a small couch on the left side wall, a fake potted plant on the floor between both.

"Sit." She points to the couch as she takes a seat behind her desk. I'm sure she feels a little more comfortable with something between us. I do as she instructs, although, being still is the last thing I want to do right now.

"Who *are* you?" Her question direct, it's meaning hitting home. How the fuck can she not remember me?

"Lucifer Sarris." I offer, then provide more context. "I'm with Devil's Halo. We're staying here for two nights. I'm the lead singer."

"Oh, you're with the rock band." She shakes her head, confusion still swirling in her eyes. "And we know each other? We've met before? Did you stay here last time you were on tour? Or for something else?"

She really doesn't have a fucking clue. I'm not sure what to do with this. So, of course, the devil on my shoulder rears its ugly horns and goes in for the kill.

"Seeing how I fucked you six times in two days, I'd like to

think we know each other. And I wanted to believe that meant you'd actually remember me, but apparently not. I guess being in the hotel business, you probably get your fair share of dick whenever you want. Especially looking like you do."

Yeah, I'm pissed, so fuck holding back.

Her face turns a ghostly white, her voice shaking when she asks her next question in a rush of words. "When? When was that?"

I scoff, unsure why I'm still humoring her with this conversation, but I tell her anyway. "October 2023. The 11th and the 12th if you want specifics." I narrow my eyes, contempt growing. "You got me noted in a diary somewhere you can reference?"

Instead of the reaction I expect from her; anger, disgust, denial, she starts to cry. Her head landing in her hands, her shoulders shaking as she begins to sob.

Well, fuck me. Not sure what's happening now or how I handle this. I sit up straight, not sure if I should get up and go to her, or wait for her to finish. Just as I make a decision and stand, she lifts her head, mascara streaking down her cheeks, the look she's giving me a startling difference from before.

"I've been trying to figure out who you are for almost two years." She blubbers out, her nose running as tears continue to cascade.

I take a couple steps closer, confusion front and center as I approach her cautiously. "I don't understand."

Her hand slides over her mouth as her eyes scrunch shut, her head shaking back and forth. When her eyes open again, she drags her fingers down her chin, so much pain on her face. "I have so many questions."

Chapter 16
Lily

All Too Well
Taylor Swift

"Not here though." I sniffle loudly, so many emotions swirling inside of me right now that I don't know which one to deal with first. I yank open drawers in my desk until I find a pack of tissues, pull several out of the package, then use them to wipe under my eyes.

"Okay." His raspy voice sounds just a few feet from me, causing me to shift my gaze up to him.

I should have known. The minute I looked at his eyes. They are all I ever see. They're squinting at me now, assessing me with concern. Which is warranted. I am acting a little like a crazy person.

"Let me get a key to a room that's free." I pull my purse from under my desk then stand. "We'll have more privacy that way."

"I have a room." He states firmly. "We can go there."

I shake my head as I walk past him, motioning for him to follow me. "I'd rather not if that's okay."

"Whatever." He mumbles as he trails behind. "Doesn't really seem like I have much of a say in this."

I pause in the hallway, twisting to face him. "I know this is strange. I promise I'll explain everything. Just, please, give me a little grace here."

His lips purse in a tight line, but he nods his acceptance at my plea. "Fine."

I stop in front of the door that opens into the check-in area. "You can wait here if you want. This will only take a second, and I understand now why you want to keep a low profile."

"Sure." He tips his forehead in acknowledgement. "Appreciate that."

"I'll be right back." I assure him before pulling the door open to walk through.

I keep my head down, moving directly to one of the computers, working quickly to find an available room. I secure it for myself, process the key, and without a word to anyone, slip back through the door to find Luc leaning against the wall.

His sunglasses are hanging from the collar of his shirt, his hands tucked into his pockets, one booted foot crossed over the other. He's turned his cap around so that the bill is facing backwards, tufts of his brown hair curling out from under the rim.

I didn't take the time to absorb anything about him earlier, but he's stunning. It's when I shift my gaze back up to his eyes that I almost suffocate on the breath I inhale. I've wondered about those eyes for so damn long. I know I'm staring but I can't seem to make myself look away.

"See something you like, Kitten?" He practically growls, and something about the way he says it causes my skin to break out in goosebumps, the hairs on the back of my neck rising.

"It's Lily." I retort, my voice a little shaky, even though I'm attempting to appear unaffected.

"Yeah, I know." He scoffs as he pushes himself off the wall. "I'm not the one who doesn't remember."

I close my eyes for a brief second, the implications of what's about to happen hitting me like a tsunami. Nothing will ever be the same after this. I take a deep breath, steel my spine, and force my feet to move. "There's an elevator down here we can use."

I sigh in relief when his heavy footsteps sound behind me, my pulse misfiring when he's suddenly beside me, matching my stride. He keeps looking over at me, contempt clearly displayed in his features. I know what I'm going to tell him is only going to increase those feelings ten-fold.

We reach the elevator, and I press the button to call it. When the doors slide open, we step inside, and I swipe the room key over the access reader, before selecting twenty-three.

"Are you fucking kidding me?" He chuffs loudly.

My eyebrows squish together as I swing my gaze to him. "What?"

"You expect me to believe that's a coincidence?" His long finger points to the number I pressed.

I assess where he's indicating, then glare over at him. "I have absolutely no idea what you're referring to."

"This just keeps getting better and better." He grumbles, his hand gripping the back of his neck as he shoots daggers toward the ceiling.

If he only knew how frustrating this was for me as well. Not having a single clue what he keeps making references to. Knowing this man holds the answers to things I didn't think I would ever know. He has so much more power over me than he even could guess.

"I'll explain everything." I promise again.

"Only reason I'm still here." He declares, one hand against the now open elevator door, as he motions for me to proceed.

I lead us to the room I procured, 2320. It's one of our suites, but it was empty, and I figured having a table and chairs, or at least any other space besides a bedroom, would be better.

"You have no idea the irony of this at all, do you?" He chuckles again, but it's not humorous. In fact, it's full of disdain.

"No one wishes I did more than you." I volley back, frustration bleeding into my tone as I toss the room key onto a side table.

His brow arches, the same side of his mouth frowning as he glances in my direction. "Where do you want to do this?"

"Table?" I suggest, pulling out one of the chairs before falling into it. He drags out the chair opposite me, settling himself across from me.

"Do you want anything?" I blurt out, realizing this could be a lengthy conversation.

"Just answers sweetheart." His response curt, all patience evaporated.

I stare across at him a moment. Wishing – wanting so badly that doing so would trigger something. Anything. But all I see, all I ever see, are his eyes. They haunt me daily, and now at least I know why.

I slide my purse off my shoulder and pull my phone out. I open my photo app, scroll a few minutes until I find what I'm looking for, and then turn the picture so he can see it. "Is this you? Us?"

His face is utterly still. His attention completely transfixed on the image I have displayed. I've looked at this picture over a thousand times. It's obviously me in the picture. My face is clear, my cheek pressed up against another. But the other person's face is hooded. Shadowed in a way that the only thing I can really see are the eyes; liquid, warm, and whiskey brown in color.

When his gaze finally shifts away, it's not to look at me, but past me, a haunted look on his face. "That was from the last time the band played in Vegas. You walked with me to the stage. We stopped on the way, and I took this selfie so you could prove to your friend that you had been hanging out with me."

"Except, you can't really see your face." I state quietly. "Even when we tried to use filter adjustments to try and lighten it."

"Are you telling me that you don't remember hanging out with me? Going to that concert with me? The day we spent together, the night after?" He fists his hands together on the table, his knuckles turning white. "Because I kind of thought our time together was pretty fucking special."

"Luc?" I sigh heavily. "Is that what I called you? Is it okay if I call you that?"

"That's my fucking name, darling." He snaps.

"I don't remember any of that." I take a deep breath and then words just spill out of me. "I was hit by a car the morning of October 13th, 2023. I was walking across Las Vegas Boulevard, and was hit by someone who ran the red light. I was in a coma for three weeks. It took me two weeks after that to even be able to talk again. When I could speak again, and tried to put the pieces together of what had happened, it was discovered that I had no memory of the accident."

I blow out another breath, noting the shock on his face, knowing it's only going to get worse from here. "As time went on, we realized I also had no memory of the three weeks prior to the accident. Nothing. It's completely gone. No matter what we try to do, nothing triggers my memories from that time. The only clues I have of what I had done, or where I had gone, were pictures on my phone, people I worked with and friends I had hung out with during that time."

I hold my phone up, the picture of us still open. "This picture, it's dated the night before my accident. So, I knew I was with someone. Doing something. But with who, and what, and where, I had no idea." I stare across the table at him. "Until now. Until you."

"Fucking hell." He exclaims, a hand scraping the hat off his head, his hair somehow still looking incredible. "You really don't remember." He shakes his head in disbelief. "All this time I thought…" His voice trails off, his hat a crumbled mess between his fingers as he stares down at it.

"We slept together then?" I probe, even though just a short time ago he had pretty clearly stated we fucked, but I needed him to say it now that he had more information from me.

His eyes dart up to mine. "Yeah." He frowns. Begins again. "Yes. Six times. If you want exact numbers. Over thirty-six hours. That's how much time we were together."

I feel my face heat at the number he just told me. *Six*

times? Either I'd lost my mind or found religion between the sheets. And with a rock star? That didn't sound like me at all.

"I know what you're thinking." His gaze boring into me as I stare across at him. "It wasn't like that." His fingers unclench from his hat and slide across the table to rest over mine. "It was special."

"How did I end up with you? Did you stay at this hotel? Is that how we met? Why didn't we exchange numbers? How could you not know my full name?" I toss questions at him faster than he can respond, but I've waited so long for these answers.

His fingers squeeze mine before he releases them and pulls them back to his side of the table. "You know that offer of something earlier? I could really use a drink."

I scoot back so fast my chair almost topples over. I'm nervous. Even more so now that I know who this man is. "Sure, of course. What do you want?"

"A bottle of tequila would be fan-fucking-tastic right now, but seeing how I have to be on stage later, how about some beer?"

"I can do that." I scurry over to the phone on a table next to the couch, and dial room service. I place an order for the beer flight we have on the menu. It has eight different bottle variations, four of each kind. I have to assume something in the mix will be what he likes. I tell them to rush the order and to place it on the house account.

When I turn around, I'm startled to find Luc just a few feet behind me, arms crossed over his chest, staring at me.

"What?" I wonder out loud why he's looking at me like he is.

"It's weird." He cocks his head analyzing me further. "Seeing you like this. Feeling like it was just yesterday.

Remembering every single detail of you. The time we spent together."

He shakes his head and begins to pace. "I was so fucking pissed at you." He stops, glancing my way. "You fucking broke me." He chuffs. "And now I find out that it's not because you ghosted me, but because you were in an accident."

He shrugs, one hand scraping through his unruly hair. "I'm not sure what to do with that now, knowing you don't remember not only me, but everything that happened between us."

"I'm sorry." I breathe out. "I wish I remembered. You have no idea how much." I take a few steps toward him, stopping a foot away. "I'm really sorry that you got hurt." I shuffle in place, trying to calm the nerves that have my pulse racing. "You said that what happened between us was different? Special?"

He nods, a slight grimace darkening his otherwise handsome face. "It was."

"How did we even meet?" I press, needing to have answers to questions that have plagued me for over a year. "I don't even like rock music."

A burst of laughter erupts from him, the smile lighting up his face making my heart skip a beat. I can certainly understand how I would have fallen for that. "What's so funny?"

"Let's sit." He strolls over to one of the sofas. "Is this okay?"

"Sure." I follow suit and sit in an arm chair that's angled so we're facing each other. I still don't know this man, even though we have a shared history, and being on the same couch doesn't feel quite right.

"What has your friend Briana told you?"

"You know Briana?" I'm shocked at this revelation.

"Not really." He leans further back into the couch, crossing his arms. "But it's how we met. Kind of." His face breaks into a wide smile as he recalls the memory. "Your friend came to our after party at Caesars, at the suite we were staying in, and you were with her."

"God, I can't imagine how she talked me into that." I murmur, knowing Bri probably held something over my head to convince me.

"Yeah," He chuckles. "That's the vibe you gave off at the party too. It was pretty clear you didn't want to be there. I actually went in pretty hard for the kill when I first saw you."

He scrapes a hand down his face, the expression a bit sheepish when he continues. "It was obvious you were out of your element. Wearing a cute little red skirt, chucks with bobby socks. It's not the usual outfit of choice for our fans."

I frown, knowing exactly which skirt he's talking about, because it's still hanging in my closet. And what was wrong with chucks? I have to wear heels all day at work. Chucks are comfy.

"Anyway." He continues, his lips tilt up in a small smile. "I was a dick. Kept taunting you every time I ran into you." His eyes shift up to meet mine. "From the first second I saw you, I thought you were gorgeous. But I also knew I was not someone you would even consider, and that kind of pissed me off, so I went on the offensive and just tried to wear you down."

"Well, you somehow ended up having sex with me, so something must have clicked." I state, wanting to know more.

"That was a complete accident." One side of his mouth

cocks up, one of his legs moving to cross over the other, his hand resting on his knee.

"What, you tripped and your dick just accidentally fell into me?" I arch a brow in defense.

"See?" He gives a small shake of his head. "This is what I love about you." He wags a finger in my direction. "You have absolutely no fear when it comes to me. You don't give two fucks that I'm famous, then or now."

"Well, if you were Morgan Wallen, I probably wouldn't be so cocky." I confess, which causes another burst of laughter from him.

"You may have mentioned him a couple times while we were together, and it was along those same lines actually."

We assess each other quietly for a few seconds, both of us lost in our own thoughts that the silence has afforded us.

"Do—"

A hard knock, followed by a loud voice, "room service" interrupts my question. He stands before I'm able to, striding to the door, tugging it wide, allowing the delivery to be wheeled into the room.

I stand when I recognize the waiter, making my way over so I can sign the slip. "Hi Colin."

"Oh, Miss Anderson." His cheeks flame a deep red, like he's caught me doing something illicit. "Didn't realize." He stammers out.

He hasn't. But I'm sure finding me in a room with a man, one who is devastatingly good looking, and famous to boot, probably has his imagination running wild.

I attempt to put his thoughts to rest. "Colin, this is Mr. Sarris. He's a guest of ours. We're discussing other room possibilities for upcoming stays."

Colin nods profusely. "Yes ma'am." Eyes popping wide

when he glances at Luc, recognition now obvious. "Nice to meet you." He manages to stutter as he continues to gawk.

"You too, man." Luc chuckles and nods. "Thanks for the beer."

"You got it." He grins, like he just delivered a trunk of gold instead. "You just let me know if you need anything else."

"Good bye, Colin." I dismiss him, holding the bill folder out in front of me. "That will be all."

"Sure, sure." I watch as he fumbles to get the door open, then backs out, bending at the waist, bowing to us both like we're royalty.

It doesn't even phase Luc. He rifles through the selection of beers until he finds one he likes, slides it out of the ice, and twists the cap off. He turns to me as he's about to take a drink, pausing when his eyes capture mine.

"What?" He lowers the bottle.

"Nothing." My eyes narrowing. "I can't imagine what it must be like to live like that. Everyone knowing who you are."

"You get used to it." He takes a long guzzle, shrugging when he's done. "You got to see that firsthand the day we hung out."

He points the bottle in my direction. "You were really good at finding places where no one gave a shit who I was."

"I still don't understand why we didn't exchange our contact information." I wonder out loud again as I walk back toward the chair, twisting to check if he's following. He is, and we both settle back into the places we were in before room service arrived.

He takes another swig from the beer, his focus fixed

completely on me. My skin prickles from the intensity of his stare.

"You had these rules." He takes a swig from the bottle, a smile appearing as he recalls and explains. "No personal information. If we decided we liked each other, we'd exchange numbers when we said goodbye."

"Except we never got to say goodbye." I realize. "Will you tell me everything, Luc?" I practically plead, desperation bleeding through my request. "Please, I need to know what happened between us in those two days."

His head moves up and down, it's slow, but it's there. His reply to my request. A breath swooshes out of me in relief, until his next sentence.

"I will, but there's something I want from you first."

Chapter 17
Luc

My Only Angel
YUNGBLUD & Aerosmith

THERE IS no way in hell I'm letting her out of my sight again until I have a way to contact her. Her and her goddamn rules are what made it impossible for me to find her two years ago. That was not going to happen again. Not now, when I finally found her. Especially now that I know the reason for her disappearance wasn't because she didn't want to see me.

"I want your number." I declare, leaning forward to set my beer on the table, then slide my phone out of my back pocket.

"Oh." Relief washes over her features, smoothing out the crinkles of concern that were present a second earlier. "Yes, that's probably a good idea."

"What's your number?" I already have a new contact window open on my phone as I fire out the demand.

"It's 702-555-2334." She recites.

I enter it, then add her first name, pausing before I enter

her last name. If only I had known this one piece of vital information two years ago. I could have found her. On Facebook, or Instagram or TikTok. Trying to find someone named Lilith or Lily from Las Vegas on socials was like trying to find a needle in a haystack. Believe me, I tried. I sigh, I think in relief, as I save her information.

"I'm going to send you a text so you'll have my number too." I inform her, glancing up at her before I do. A second later, a buzzing vibrates on the table.

"Now?" Her soft voice has me diverting my attention from my phone to her face. "Will you tell me?"

"You don't remember anything?" I set my phone on the table, snagging the beer back in my hand.

"I only know what I've been told." She shakes her head, her hands folded in her lap. "Camera footage from the lights show that I was in the crosswalk, that I definitely had the walk signal, and that a car drove directly into me, not putting any brakes on until after I was struck. I was hit on my right side. My femur and four ribs were broken. When I hit the pavement, my skull was fractured, which resulted in the head trauma suppressing or causing my memory loss."

"Jesus, Lily." I slam the beer down on the table as I stand, wanting to comfort her somehow, but not knowing what the limits are. "That must have been awful."

She shrugs, a frown marring her otherwise perfect face. "I don't remember any of it, and I did a lot of healing the weeks I was in the coma. By the time I woke up, I wasn't really in any pain."

She pauses a moment before continuing. "It turns out that the driver was drunk. Not that it makes any real difference, but I got a large settlement that covered all my medical bills with a lot to spare."

"I'm really sorry that happened to you." I walk over to grab another beer, and remember my manners. "Sorry, did you want one of these?"

"No, I'm good." She watches me, her gaze assessing as I go back to my spot on the couch. "I have a video."

She stands now, talking as she goes over to the table. "Of the accident. It's from the red-light camera. The police had to surrender it to me as part of my settlement for the lawyers."

She comes over and sits down next to me. "Do you want to see it?"

Do I? Not sure I want to see her getting hit by a car. But she seems to want to share it with me for whatever reason, so I shrug. "If you want me to."

She takes a second to scroll through her album, handing the phone to me as the video begins to play. "There's no sound." She explains I take it from her, my eyes glued to the screen.

It's grainy and in black and white. A weird feeling creeps over my skin when I see her in the dress she had been wearing the day we spent together. The little chucks on her feet.

I squint, then use my fingers to zoom in to see what she's carrying, my breath catching when I do. It's a tray, with two coffees and a white paper bag. She *had* gone to get coffee. She was coming back. Something shifts inside of me, and all of the anger, the months and months of rage I lived on, just slip away. She was coming back to me.

In the next second, a car slams into her, her body flying through the air before landing back on the road, and I recoil at the shock of it, almost dropping the phone. I stop the video and hand her phone back. I've seen everything I need to.

"I-" I shake my head, lost for words. I don't know what to say, so instead, I wrap my arms around her and pull her into a hug. The feel of her against me, her smell, her soft frame, all things I never thought I was going to experience again. It's a mind-fuck, and it's taking me a beat to come to terms with everything.

There are people you get over. People who fade like old songs you don't replay. And then, there was her. Her memory was like a bruise I couldn't stop poking. A wound I never wanted to heal, no matter what I may have tried to tell myself. Some hearts don't heal, don't move on. They wait. And I realize as I'm holding her, I waited. I never fucking stopped.

She's stiff for a few seconds, but then relaxes, her hands sliding up to rest on my shoulders. It's like we both finally have some of the answers we've been looking for and a huge weight has been lifted. She draws back after a moment, shifting a foot away from me, but staying on the couch.

"Sorry." Her mouth curves into a small frown. "It's a strange thing, knowing we spent time together, slept together, yet have no memory of it and can tell that it meant something to you."

"To us." I correct her. "We both wanted to keep seeing each other. Even if it was after my tour ended."

"I believe you." She nods, a sad expression on her face. "Can you tell me what we did, where we went?"

I tell her everything, starting with finding her in my room, going to her apartment, what happened in her apartment, going to Mt. Charleston, driving her car, the Peppermill, the concert, the suite after. I tell her what our rules were, getting a little laugh from her when I tell her about my request for her to wear a dress. I share every single detail with her. And then more. The things she wouldn't know.

"When I woke up and you were gone, I lost it." I grimace as I recall my behavior back then. "I didn't know I could fall for someone that quickly, but it seems I did."

I glance over at her, not surprised in the least that her damn lower lip is clenched between her teeth. "I tried every-thing I could think of to find you. Went back to that restau-rant, even tried calling Uber. And Dean had hooked up with your friend, but he doesn't get attached, even a little, so that was a dead end."

"Should have checked the hospitals." She laughs weakly at her own joke. "Trying to retrace my steps wasn't any better."

She shakes her head. "I didn't know where my car was for almost two months after I got out of the hospital. And then, one day, I went through the bag the hospital had given me, and there was a valet ticket and a hotel key for Caesars."

She rolls her eyes as she continues. "I tried to get them to tell me who the key had originally been registered to, but they couldn't. The key had been deactivated somehow." She smiles. "I did get my car back though, and that was one hell of a tip I had to leave."

"I wrote an entire album of songs about you." I counter, just laying it all out on the line now. "All about how much I loved and loathed you at the same time."

Her brow shoots up. "Love?"

"I don't know." I confess. "I think so. Didn't actually believe that could happen in less than two days, but also don't think I would have gone as crazy as I did, unless it was."

"I wish I could remember." She whispers. "Anything. Just one little bit of something."

"I know it's wrong to admit, but at least I know you not coming back, not being there when I woke up, wasn't because you were trying to flee the scene."

I feel like a complete shit bag for saying it out loud, and as soon as the words are out of my mouth, I want to reel them back in. She got hit by a damn car. She had broken bones. She was in the hospital for weeks.

The thought of her being hurt at all guts me. I'd rather take the pain I suffered, again, if it meant it would give her back her memory and take away what she went through.

"Fuck, I'm sorry, Lily." I fist my hand and thump it against my forehead. "That was stupid to say."

"It's okay." She lets out a weary sigh. "You're being honest. It's okay that you felt, or feel, confused. This is a lot to take in."

I stare hard, because even though I am sorry, she needs to know what she meant to me. "Stupid, not blind. I still want what I want."

My phone buzzes in my pocket, and I slide it out to see who it is. "Shit." It's from Dean wondering where I am. I didn't realize it had gotten so late. "I have to go get ready for the show tonight." I explain, looking over at her, not ready to leave her yet.

"Where is it?" She stands, smoothing down her shirt as she does.

"The Sphere." I state. "It's a pretty big show for us. We're playing tonight and tomorrow."

"Yeah," she nods. "That's an amazing venue to play in."

"Do you want to go?" I toss out, trying not to cringe at the desperation in my voice.

"Oh, well." She pauses, looking down at her phone for a

minute. "I can't. I didn't realize how long we'd been talking, and I actually need to be somewhere."

"How about tomorrow?" I press, wanting to try and figure out if there's a way to recapture what we had two years ago. "Can I see you again?"

"Yes." She agrees more quickly than I expected. "I have tomorrow off. Do you think you could come to me?"

"Yeah, of course." I don't hesitate at the opportunity to spend more time with her. "Shoot me an address." I point to her phone. "You have my number now."

"Okay." She glances at her phone again. "Is ten too early?"

"Lily, I'll come any damn time that works for you. I just want to spend more of it with you."

I want so badly to grab her face in my hands and kiss her. Taste her. Feel every inch of her. Now that she's in front of me, it's like she was never gone. Her not knowing who I am though is surreal. I know I have to take a damn minute and let her catch up.

"Be careful what you wish for." She warns, as she starts walking toward the door.

"What's that supposed to mean?" Not sure how to react to the comment.

"A lot has changed since those two days we spent together." Her hand is on the knob, her body turning toward mine, her expression somber.

"I just-" She pauses, takes a deep breath. "Let's just talk about it tomorrow, okay? We've already covered so much today."

"Tomorrow." I confirm with a nod, then follow her out of the room.

Chapter 18
Lily

Change
YUNGBLUD

I PACE NERVOUSLY BACK and forth in my kitchen. It's a quarter to ten, and I have no doubt that Luc will be here right on time, if not early. It was quite clear he wanted to spend more time with me.

I googled him last night. I knew I probably shouldn't. I didn't want it to influence my own organic opinion of him. But after wondering about who the man in the photo was for so long, I had to know more about him.

The things I read weren't pretty; bad boy, reckless behavior, hard drinking and drug use. Endless pictures of him, always with his arm slung over a different woman's shoulder or with his band. Everything I read seemed in such contrast to the man I met yesterday.

I close my eyes, my head falling back on my shoulders as I say a silent prayer. What happens today is really going to change everything. I heave out a breath, open my eyes, and then almost shriek when there's a knock on the door. Yep, he's early. I knew he would be.

Here goes nothing. I inhale another breath for courage and stride over to the door, pulling it open. He's stunning. It's the first thing that enters my brain when my eyes land on him.

He's dressed simply, in faded blue jeans, a white t-shirt and a pair of sneakers. No hat on this time, his sunglasses pushed up on his head instead. His hair is messy, but it's in that way a guy that looks like him can get away with and have it look perfect.

"Hey." His hand lands on the door frame above my head as he greets me. "You moved."

"That's right," I recall from our conversation yesterday. "You came to my apartment." I stand back from the open door and motion for him to come inside. "I needed more space."

"This is nice." He offers, as he steps inside and openly assesses my home. It's really not anything special, but it is nicer than the apartment I had.

It's a small house, with a couple bedrooms, a large open living space, and has a yard. And it's in a gated community, which I love. It offers a little bit more security.

The settlement I got from the accident made it possible for me to buy the house almost outright, so the mortgage is actually less than my rent had been. And I still have my dad's car, which meant no car payment.

I probably could afford to work a job less demanding than the one I have at Sapphire Resorts, but I really do love my job. And they were amazing to me when I was in the accident. I don't think I cooked a meal for almost three months after I was home.

"Did you want to do something today?" He's standing at

the edge of my living room, one hand in his pocket as he asks the question.

"I actually have something else I want to talk to you about."

"Oh, okay." He nods, watching as I walk toward the kitchen, my bare feet pattering against the tile floor as I step into that space.

"Do you want something to drink?" I point to the counter. "I've got coffee, or water or juice?"

"Coffee actually sounds good." He scrapes a hand over the brown beard lining his chin. "Only been up about an hour. Ended up being a later night than I expected."

"Oh, how was the show?" I spit out, embarrassed I didn't think to ask already. "Was playing at the Sphere cool?"

"So fucking cool." A wide grin breaks across his face, pure joy shining from him. "We've played all sorts of venues, but that place is unreal." He gives a small shake of his head. "In the best way."

"You want cream or sugar?" I place a mug in the Keurig and press the button to start the brew, then switch gears back to his show. "I went to see the Eagles there back in March, and it was amazing."

"The Eagles are amazing anywhere they play." He concurs, glancing toward the mug of coffee. "Black is perfect."

The coffee finishes and I carry the mug over to him. "You want to sit in the living room?" He nods as he takes it from me, his lips parting to blow a breath across the dark liquid before taking a sip as he follows me.

"Did you tell the guys in the band about me?" I'm curious what they must think. Especially after what he told me yesterday. I'm sure they're worried what finding me might do to him.

We both sit on the couch, each choosing a corner. "I told them." He's quiet a moment, his gaze darting around the room before landing on me again. "It's part of the reason I was up so late. Didn't get a chance to break the news until after the show." He shrugs. "They had questions." He chuckles. "Lots of questions."

"Hey!" He exclaims with a smile as Teddy appears out of nowhere, jumping up beside him on the couch. "I remember you."

He scratches at the scruff under the cat's neck, loud purrs beginning to rumble from Teddy. He only stays a second, departing as quickly as he came, tail wagging in the air as he does.

Luc takes another drink from the cup as he watches Teddy leave. "Dean wanted to come with me today. Make sure I would be okay." One side of his mouth quirks up. "They have a right to be worried. I didn't handle things well, when-" He clears his throat, "when I couldn't find you."

"I'm sorry if this is making things harder for you." I shift on the couch so my body is facing him. "Harder with the band."

"It's not your fault, Lily." He shakes his head. "For whatever reason, the universe had different plans for us two years ago, but it seems fate brought us back together anyway."

His eyes narrow as he stares over at me. "I have to believe there's a reason for that."

Oh, there's a reason alright, and I know I can't put off telling him much longer. "So, you said we slept together a few times during the two nights we were together?"

"Yep." The 'p' popping at his confirmation.

"Did we use protection?" I can feel my face heating and hate how my body always betrays me. It shouldn't be a question that causes me to blush.

His brows draw together at my question, and I don't think it's in confusion, but rather maybe because he's wondering why I would ask. "Actually, we didn't."

His eyes narrow as he analyzes me. "You were going to go and get the Plan B pill in the morning…" His frame tenses as he sits up straight. "Except you got hit by a car."

"Yeah," I repeat like a robot. "Except I got hit by a car."

"Holy shit, Lily." He stands abruptly, coffee splashing out of the mug as he does. "Are you trying to tell me what I think you are?"

I rise as well, but much slower, the words I'm about to say weighing me down. My heart is thundering under my rib cage, my nerves causing my hands to shake as I feel my head bob up and down as I begin to explain.

"I didn't even realize until four months after the accident." The words come out in a rush, and I almost stop when he turns a ghostly shade of white, but I keep going, wanting to get this over with. "I hadn't gotten my period, but I thought it was because my body was broken and healing. My boobs hurt, but my ribs were broken, so I just attributed it to that."

"You were pregnant." He surmises, his eyes flicking to my stomach, like the baby is still inside me.

"When I realized my abdomen wasn't swollen, but indeed growing, I went to my doctor and yes, they confirmed it." I nod and say it again. "I was pregnant. Almost seventeen weeks by the time I realized."

"I think I might throw up." His hand moves over his stomach as he walks toward the kitchen, placing the coffee on the island as he heads to the sink. "I can't fucking believe this."

I watch as he places both hands on the edge of the sink, his head falling between his arms, his chest heaving up and down.

I understand how he feels. It's about the same way I reacted. Worse because I didn't even remember who I had sex with. Had no idea who the father of my baby was.

I walk up behind him and gently begin to rub small circles on his back with my fingers. "I'm sorry, Luc." I whisper. I know I just changed his life forever, and I have absolutely no idea what this is going to do to him.

"I'm okay." He murmurs, his back vibrating under my touch. "I just wasn't expecting that."

"Imagine how I felt when I found out." I say softly. "At least you remember having sex with me."

He whirls around, my balance thrown off by the quick action, and he grips me around the arm to steady me. "Jesus Christ, that's true." He closes his eyes for a second. "This is so fucked up."

"Just a little." I agree, our eyes locking when his lids open.

"Did you have the baby?" He asks, his voice low.

"I did." I nod. "I had a little girl. On July 4th, last year. She's almost a year old."

He stares at me, with the very same eyes that our daughter has. The ones that have haunted me for the last eleven months. So very different from my light blue colored irises. She has his hair, his eyes, even his nose. It's uncanny. And so strange after wondering for so long who her father might be.

"I have a daughter." He repeats, as if saying the words will make it more real for him.

"Only if you want one." I say, knowing that there is nothing normal about this situation.

He takes a step back as if slapped. "Wait, what?"

"Luc, you didn't ask for this." I throw my hands up.

"Neither did you." He retorts, anger in his tone.

"I just mean that I don't expect anything from you. I didn't even know who you were until yesterday. I didn't know if I'd ever find out who her father was. I assumed I'd always be her only parent."

"But you're not." He takes a step closer to me. "I'm her father." He shakes his head. "Even if I didn't know it until five minutes ago. I would never not acknowledge a child that's mine, let alone walk away."

"I-" I turn, twisting to hide the tears that come unannounced, my shoulders beginning to shake at the emotions I'm trying to contain.

"Lily." Luc pulls me to him, enveloping me in his arms, his breath warm against my ear. "Please don't cry."

I try to stop, I really do, but the more I try, the more I seem to leak tears. I let him hold me. It's really, really nice to not feel so alone.

When I can finally speak, I peek up at him under my wet lashes. "I just never thought I would find her father. Or that when I did, he would want to be involved in her life."

"Here I am." He assures me, not an ounce of hesitation in his response.

"Here you are." I say, disbelief still surging through me.

"Lily?" He peers down at me.

"Yes?"

"Do you think I could meet my daughter?"

"Of course." I laugh, nodding through the tears still escaping in little bursts as I step out of his embrace. "Her name is Larkin, by the way. Larkin Marie. And she looks exactly like you."

"Larkin." He says the name out loud.

"It's kind of after Larkspur. It's the flower for the month of July." I shrug. "I'm a Lily, so I figured another flower in my garden. And Marie is my mom's name."

"I like it. It's pretty." He offers me a smile. "Where is she?" He looks around. "Is she here?"

"She's at my mom's." I explain. "I wasn't sure how this was going to go, so I dropped Larkin off with her earlier."

"Can we go see her?" He persists. "Is it far?"

"Let me call my mom. I'll have her bring Larkin here." I grab my phone off the counter. "She's only a few miles away. She helps me a lot. It's been good for her. It's filled a big hole for her. With my dad gone."

"God." He clutches onto the back of his neck, the expression on his face one of disbelief. "I'm a dad."

"You're taking this much better than I thought you would."

"I think I'm still in shock actually." He admits. "I thought running into you yesterday, finding you after two years; I thought nothing could surprise me more." He chuckles. "You sure blew that to hell."

"There's so much we still need to figure out." I remind him.

"And we will." He points to my phone. "Call your mom. I want to meet my daughter."

Chapter 19
Luc

Dad
Michele Morrone

I HAVE A FUCKING KID. Mind blown. Not the news I was expecting to get today, or anytime in the immediate future if I was being honest with myself. If I'm being one hundred percent real, when I originally met Lily, it was the first time I had even considered the possibility of dating anyone long term, but those thoughts never strayed further than that.

Having kids? Maybe one day, but not something I had pondered at all. Shit, I was thirty. Plenty old enough to be a dad. Except that most of the time, I still act like the rockstar I am, and pull shit I probably shouldn't at my age. Guess having a daughter just put growing up into overdrive for me.

We still had over thirty dates left on our tour, which was supposed to run through August. I had no idea how I was going to try to be a father while I was on the road. The guys were going to freak the fuck out over this news. I was tempted to text them right now, but knew it was news that needed to be told in person. Had a feeling tonight was going to be another late one.

"You doing okay?" It's Lily, coming back into the living room after stepping away for a few minutes to call her mom.

"Yeah." I confirm. "Just thinking about what this is going to mean for the band." I provide more information so she can follow where my head is at. "Me being on tour."

Her face scrunches, her head tilting. "You think the guys won't want you to be in the band anymore?"

I can't help it, I laugh out loud. That would *never* happen. As dysfunctional as we all may be, we're a family. And I know without a doubt, they will accept Larkin with open arms.

"No, no, it's not that." I offer her a tentative smile. "I'm on tour through August. I'm trying to work out how I can spend time with you and Larkin. I don't want to have to wait another two months." I give a slight shake of my head. "I feel like I've already lost so much time."

"Oh." Although her expression relaxes, I can tell she's rolling what I just dropped around in her mind.

"We'll figure it out Lily." I don't want her to overthink it, but the band is supposed to leave tomorrow morning. Our next show is in L.A. two days from now. I can technically take a flight out, instead of travelling on the bus with the guys, giving me an extra day here to try and convince her to do what I already know I want to happen. I need to talk to the guys first about everything. Make sure they are on board with what I have in mind.

She's pacing, back and forth, again and again, in front of the television mounted against the far wall. She has to be nervous. So much new information to process over the last twenty-four hours.

I want to do something to ease her concerns, her fears, the apprehension she has to be experiencing right now, but I don't know what that is. I usually fuck or drink my way out of most situations. Don't think that's going to work this time.

"Lily." I stand and amble closer to her, stopping when I'm an arms-length away, reaching a hand out to stop her. She stops in place, her eyes swinging to mine, the look in them a little wild. "It's going to be okay."

"Is it?" She questions out loud. "I'm not so sure." She huffs out a breath, crossing her arms. "This is all starting to hit really hard."

"I know." I say, keeping my voice soft. 'It's a lot."

"I mean, Jesus Christ on a cracker." She exclaims with a shake of her head. "You're a rockstar. An actual, for real, bigger than life, rockstar! What was I thinking? I can't believe of all the people that could have been Larkin's father, it's a famous rockstar."

A deranged kind of laughter leaves her as a hand clamps over her mouth as she stares at me, like it's the first time she's seeing me.

I take a large step forward, closing the gap between us and grip her forearms gently to tug her close. Her icy blue eyes lock on my face, her hand falling away from her mouth, my attention diverted now to her lips, so pink, so full.

"Lily." My voice is gravelly as I say her name, so I clear my throat, swallowing to try and tamp down the desire that has sparked to life inside me. "I promise it's going to be okay."

"How can you possibly promise that?" She breathes out, our bodies so close together that I feel the warm moisture from her breath as she speaks.

"Because there is nothing I wouldn't do to make sure that's the case." I lick my lips, wanting so badly to press them against hers. Her gaze flits to my mouth, back to my eyes, and then back to my mouth again, and I know that she's thinking about kissing me as well.

She's back in my life like a storm. Messy, dangerous and impossible to ignore. I should hate her for the turmoil she's causing, for the time we've lost. But I can't. I never could. And it's why I'm standing here, with my heart in my hands, waiting for the lightning to hit again. And it will. I have no doubt because it always did with us.

I lean in, so ready to taste her again after two years of yearning for her, my pulse racing beneath my skin as my temperature rises.

"Luc…" She whispers, not pulling back, instead tilting her head up.

"Hello!" The door opens as the greeting rings out, both of us stepping away from the other in a rush. "We're here!"

We break apart, I think both of us realizing just in the nick of time that we were about to do something reckless. I rake a hand through my hair, my nerves zinging to life under my skin, knowing I'm about to meet my daughter.

Her mother, an older clone of her daughter, appears before us, her hands gripped firmly around the handle of an infant car seat. It feels like a thousand butterfly wings are fluttering against my insides as my heart rate increases.

"So, you're the one." Her mother states, as she assesses me, scanning me from head to toe.

"It would seem." I nod, taking a few tentative steps in her direction, eager to see my daughter.

"Well, it's obvious who she looks like now." Her lips lift

just a fraction as she glances from the seat to me. "And we have always said she's a beautiful baby."

A backwards compliment? I think that's a good sign?

"Mom, you said you would behave." Lily strolls up to her mother and relieves her of the car seat, twisting it around so I can finally see inside of it.

She's asleep. Her tiny mouth is scrunched up in a pucker, her brow furrowed, like she's aware of the tension in the room, but choosing to try and hide from it.

Her hair is the exact same color as mine, little curls sprouting in all directions on her head. Her skin is the palest pink, and so smooth. She's so little. And, she's the most beautiful thing I've ever seen.

I don't take my eyes off of her as Lily sets the seat on the couch and begins to unbuckle the straps around her. She starts to squirm, a little sound of protest at being disturbed squeaking from her.

"You're okay baby girl." Lily coos to her as she lifts her out of the seat, her body starting to sway back and forth as she cradles Larkin against her chest. She flashes a smile my way. "Come meet your daughter."

I tread over, my steps slow, not wanting to startle the baby. When I'm inches from them, I freeze in place and just stare at this little miracle that's suddenly in my life. She's chewing on her thumb, her eyes, the exact same color as mine, blink as they assess me.

I rouse my courage to feather my fingers over her head, the locks downy soft, then trail them down further to stroke over the skin of her face. She smiles at me then, her cheek lifting underneath my touch, a dimple appearing, and I'm transported to another realm I didn't know existed. One where only pure, unconditional love exists.

My heart expands so much that I have to suck in a breath, which I realize a second later, is a gasp escaping. How did the world I know exist without this perfect little human?

I blink up at Lily, feeling the tears track down the planes of my face and into my beard before I understand they are falling. "She's so perfect."

"She is." Lily's face beams as she looks between me and Larkin. "Do you want to hold her?"

"Can I?" My voice raising an octave as I take a step back.

Laughter bubbles from Lily, prompting Larkin to giggle as well, and the sound just floors me. The laughter from my child is the most beautiful sound I have ever heard. Until I hear her speak.

"Mama." Her tiny hand reaching out to touch Lily's parted lips, and my heart explodes.

"Hi baby." She kisses the tips of Larkin's fingers. "Did you have fun with Grandma?"

"She was so good."

I had completely forgotten about her mother. I was so transfixed on Larkin. She's next to Lily now, smiling down at her granddaughter as she begins to talk to her in a baby voice. "I'm going to go now though. I think Mommy will be fine."

She glances up at me as she completes her sentence, directing her attention to me now. "She will be, right?"

"Of course." I assure her, nodding my affirmation. "Completely fine. I'm not here to cause any problems."

"I checked you and that band out online." Her eyes narrowing. "You know that's not any kind of life for a baby?"

"Yes, ma'am." I scratch at my chin, my nerves raw by this point. "I wouldn't-" I pause for a second to collect my thoughts. "I understand."

"Let's hope so." She graces me with a tight smile. "Lily has been through enough."

"Mom." Lily admonishes with an eye roll. "Enough. Luc didn't even know about any of this until thirty minutes ago."

"Well, maybe if he treated you like a lady, instead of a tramp, and gotten your number, that wouldn't have been the case." She retorts, crossing her arms.

"Mom." Lily chides. "I thought I explained to you this morning that we had every intention of exchanging numbers, I just got hit before that could happen."

She shakes her head, absently sliding Larkin into my arms, my eyes popping wide as I stare down at the bundle I'm now holding, as Lily continues to argue with her mom. Any noise from them is silenced as I behold the wonder I'm staring down at.

"Hi Larkin." I murmur softly to her. "I'm your dad."

Her eyes latch onto mine, her smile gummy as she beams up to investigate me. I adjust her in my arms, marveling at how absolutely precious and small she is.

"You might be the prettiest girl I've even seen." I trace a finger down her arm, her little fist grasping onto it when I reach her hand. Little does she know, that hold is one I'm going to treasure and cherish forever.

"I'm sorry about that, Luc." Lily's hand on my arm grabs my attention a moment later. "She's just being protective."

I look around and realize her mom isn't here anymore.

"You don't have to apologize." I tell her. "I like that she's protective of you. It's a sign of a good mom. She loves you."

"Thank you for understanding." Her face softens as she takes us in. Me and Larkin. "She looks good on you."

"Who would have thought?" I chuff, startling Larkin. "Sorry little one."

"So, now what?" She throws out the question that's been running like a train through my thoughts since I found her yesterday.

"I guess that's what we have to figure out."

Chapter 20
Luc

Right Now
Van Halen

"SAY THAT AGAIN?" Dean leans forward, propping his elbows on his knees as he does, like being closer to me will make what I just said any different.

"Lily had a baby, and it's mine." I repeat, saying it slow and loud so there's no confusion.

"Is this a fucking joke?" Mikey spits out as he rises from the couch, throwing a hand in the air. "You don't see this chick for two years and you're just going to believe some baby she had is yours?"

I slide my phone out of my back pocket and open a photo of Larkin I took earlier today, turning it so he can see the screen.

"Think I can deny this?" I arch a brow.

His eyes pop wide, his hand fisting a clump of his hair. "Holy fuck."

"Yeah." I concur with a dip of my chin. "She looks exactly like me."

"Let me see." Dean extends his arm toward my phone, so I give it to him. After a second, he shakes his head. "Well, damn, brother. Should we get some cigars?" He hands the phone back to me.

"Think it's kind of late for that." I mutter, shoving my cell back in my pocket.

"So, what does this mean for you and the band?" Hayden, ever the practical one, finally chimes in.

I shrug as I take a load off in a chair, kicking my bare feet up on the table. "Trying to figure that out, but wanted to fill you in first."

"Have you told Mom or Dad yet?" Mikey takes a swig out of the tequila bottle he's holding after he asks me the question.

"Nope." I scrape my fingers through my hair, still wet from the shower I took after our show. "Wanted to share it with guys first."

"They're going to fucking flip over this." A wicked grin spreads across his face. "I wanna be in the room for that call."

"Fuck off, Mikey." Dean comes to my defense before I have a chance to respond to my asshat of a brother. "Think he needs that additional stress right now?"

I swing a glance in Dean's direction and shoot him a silent thanks, and then address my brother. "They'll be fine. Probably will be over the moon that one of us is actually giving them a grandchild."

"Won't fucking be me, that's for sure." He scoffs, pacing, bottle still dangling from his fingers. He's going to need a liver transplant by the time he's thirty-five at the rate he's going.

"And thank that same God for that blessing." I punch back. "One of you in this world is enough."

"You're such an asshole, Luc. Always thinking you're so fucking special." He stops to face me, pointing the bottle in my direction. "Believe it was you who ran our last damn tour into the ground. And oh yeah, what a fucking surprise, over this same chick!"

I jump to my feet and surge toward him, Dean somehow between us before I can throw a fist in the fucker's face.

"Whoa!" Dean yells out. "Enough of this shit!" He pushes me with more force than I expect and I stumble back, pinwheeling my arms to catch my balance. "We're not doing this with you two again."

He jams a finger in Mikey's chest. "Shut your big mouth and go sit over there." He points to a chair that's far enough away from where I was sitting that we can't reach each other.

As I turn to sit, I almost run into Hayden. Always quiet, but always there. Our strong and steady. "You good?" He inquires quietly.

I nod. "I'm chill."

My heart is thundering in my chest, but I go back to where I was sitting and force myself to settle back in. Dean and Hayden do the same.

"Now let's see if we can behave, act like the adults we are, and have a civil conversation about this." Dean directs a hard look in Mikey's direction. "You feel me?"

"Whatever." He grumbles, taking another large swig from the bottle.

"I'd like to ask her to come on tour with us." I toss out, everyone's gaze landing on me, shock evident on each face. I give them a second to process what I just suggested.

"I want to get to know my own child. I don't want to have

to put it off another two months." I blow out a heavy sigh, trying to slow the bouncing of my heart. "I've already missed her first year."

"You want to take a baby on tour?" Mikey's expression doesn't hide his disdain. "With us? Are you fucking serious?"

"As a heart attack." I state. "I know it means we'll have to make some changes." My jaw clenches as I dart my gaze to each one of the guys. "This is something I really need to happen."

"I'm not riding with some baby on a bus for hours. Thing probably cries all the time." Mikey, ever the agreeable one chimes in.

"Larkin." I practically growl, wanting to throttle him. "Her name is Larkin, and you are her damn uncle, so you better fucking find a way to deal, little brother."

"Maybe we can get you your own bus." Dean suggests, before I can act on the impulses pertaining to Mikey. "We're going to have to loop Cherry in to see if that's possible. Maybe she can get another bus for us in L.A.?"

"Yeah, let's see what she can do." I fold my hands in front of me, grateful that Dean's got his head on straight. Cherry's our tour manager and has a way of making the impossible possible.

"I can do that for you, Luc." Hayden offers, and I thank him. "Just as a side note, that reporter from Amped is supposed to join us on tour once we're in Portland. Are you planning on going public with the news that you have a daughter?"

"Fuck." I sigh. "I forgot about that, but I definitely don't want this shit out there yet. This adjustment is going to be hard enough on Lily as it is."

"I can talk to PR tomorrow and see what they suggest." Hayden advises.

"Appreciate that so much man." I nod to him.

"I have a question for you." Mikey chimes in again. "Have you asked Lily if she wants to do this?"

"Not yet." I frown. Can't be mad at him this time, cause calling me out on this shit is spot on. "I wanted to run it by you first to make sure it would be okay."

"Like what we want or think really fucking matters." He chuffs in anger. "You'll do whatever you want like you always do."

"Can you just stop being an asshole for five minutes?" I stand again, but don't charge like I want to. "You think this is an easy situation for me to be in? Could you, just for once, be a decent fucking human being?"

He shrugs, locking angry eyes with me, slugging from the tequila in response. Fucking dick.

"We're supposed to take off in the morning." Hayden interjects, trying to break through some of the tension in the room. "What is your plan?"

"Yeah," I sit before continuing. "I'm going to stay here another day to see if I can work this out with Lily. I'll fly out to L.A. in time for our show." I scratch my chin. "Hopefully Lily and Larkin will be with me."

"And if not?" Dean asks, and I know it's not to be confrontational, but because they all need to know I'm not going to lose it on them like last time.

"I'll be okay." I promise, meeting them all in the eye as I look around the room. "Not gonna crash and burn again. She may not give me the answer I want, and if that's the case, then I'll figure out ways to see them in between our show dates. It'll be harder, but I'll do what I have to."

"That can't happen again man." Dean is referring to my epic fallout after I couldn't find Lily last time we were here.

"It won't."

I'm going to get her back.

This devil fell for an angel, only to discover she had the ability to make hell burn brighter.

Chapter 21
Lily

Head's Carolina, Tail's California
Jo Dee Messina

"You want me to do what?" My mouth hanging open in disbelief at Luc's request.

"I know it sounds crazy, but it's not. It won't be. I promise." The plea that falls from his lips so full of desperation, I almost say yes immediately. Almost.

"Luc, I can't drop my entire life at a moment's notice to follow you around on tour."

"Join me on tour." He corrects as he takes my hand in his, wrapping his fingers around mine. "Not following me. We'd have a whole bus to ourselves, so plenty of privacy and room for you and Larkin."

"I have a job. Larkin has a schedule. I have a home. The only one she knows." All facts that are important to the life I've worked really hard to provide for my daughter.

"Take a leave of absence. We can keep her on her schedule. And we'll make the bus a home for her. Make sure she

157

has all her things. Everything she needs. I can pay for your house expenses while you're away." He counters, an answer for every concern I have.

"Luc, this is too much, too fast, too soon." I snake my hand back, wringing it with my other as I shake my head. "We don't even know each other. Not really."

"That's what I'm trying to change." He states like it's really that simple.

"I can't." My head swinging back and forth with my response.

"Why?" He peppers back. "Tell me three good reasons. Because the last three you tried, I already gave you solutions to."

"You just expect me to walk away from my entire life and immerse myself in yours?" I throw my hands up in the air with a huff. "You're crazy."

"Maybe." He murmurs, stepping closer to me. "Lily, you were never even mine to lose, but I lost you all the same. I thought about you so much that I wondered if you could feel it. And yes, it would be so much easier for me to walk away, to not care. But our souls found each other again. I have to believe there's a reason for that."

"Luc…"

Jesus. I think he just stole a piece of my heart with that speech.

"Just say yes." He is practically begging me and yet, I still can't find it in me to say the word he is asking for.

"It's easy to see how I could have spent two days with you. Slept with you." I muse out loud, my mouth quirking down in one corner as I openly assess him, listing off the obvious reasons. "You're gorgeous. You know how to work your charm. You know all the right things to say."

He says nothing, just crosses his arms and leans against my kitchen counter, waiting for me to continue.

"*That* me wants to say yes. Wants to hang out with the incredibly cool rockstar and live life on the road and see what could happen."

"But?" His lips purse into a tight line.

"The mother in me is screaming at me to run. Screaming for me to keep my daughter away from that life, from-"

He cuts me off, pointing to himself, "me?"

"No." I shake my head. I wasn't saying this the correct way. "I wouldn't do that to you. Or to her. I want my child to know who her father is."

"Don't *you* want to know who her father is, too?" He asks softly.

"It's not that simple." I exclaim, groaning in frustration.

"It's as simple or as difficult as you want it to be." His response curt.

"Do you have any idea what a day in the life of a one-year-old is like?" I snap back at him.

"No." He drawls, pushing off the counter to come closer to me, his voice low. "But I would very much like to, hence this request."

I close my eyes and shake my head, just looking at him making it that much harder to stay firm in my decision.

"Lily." He's close enough that I can feel the heat coming from his body. "Look at me."

I open my lids and stare across at him. *Ugh. Those damn eyes.*

"Give me one week." He holds up a single finger. "If it's not working, if Larkin can't adjust, or you and I discover we can't stand each other, then you can go home."

He sighs tiredly. "It's all I'm asking. Just one week. I've

already missed the first eleven months of her life. I don't want to miss anymore."

Christ on a cracker. That was like a knife to the heart. I couldn't imagine going more than two days without my girl. I should be jumping for joy that this man, this man who had no idea until yesterday he even had a daughter, wants to be her father. Wants to spend time with her, with us. It's what I have prayed for a thousand times and more.

Why then was I fighting against this so hard? Was it because of the band? Or who he is? Or was it more than that? Was I afraid to share Larkin after her belonging only to me for so long? Or was I afraid of what he could also mean to me?

"Can I think about it?" It's the best I can do right now and I owe him that much.

"Yes, of course." A wide smile breaks across his face, and it's surreal to see the same dimple in his cheek that my daughter has. "I have to fly to L.A. for our show tomorrow night no matter what. But if you need more time, then okay."

"Just give me a day." I finally concede, unable to not match the smile he's beaming at me.

"Thank you!" His hand is suddenly cupping my cheek, his lips pressing against mine, the action so unexpected and quick I barely have time to react. But I do. An electric current zaps all the way down to my toes and I find myself leaning into him to return the kiss, my fingers clenching the material of his t-shirt.

And then, he's gone, cold space between us, his eyes wide as he takes two steps away from me. "I'm sorry. I didn't-"

"It's okay." I bow my head, my cheeks flaming at my own reaction to him. When I swing my gaze back up to him, his fingers are brushing over his lips.

Yep, it was real. And holy hell, now I know why I slept with him so many times in such a short time. That was barely anything and I swear to all things holy, there's a heat at my core I haven't felt since before my accident.

"Larkin should be awake any minute from her nap." I stride over to the baby monitor on another counter, praying for it to squawk to life and save me from trying to make small talk with Luc.

"I didn't mean to make you uncomfortable." His voice gravely as he stands statue still.

"You didn't." I lie, not making any kind of eye contact so he can't read right through me, busying myself with washing a cup in the sink.

"It's just-" He pauses, a sigh sounding before he continues. "I forget sometimes. That you don't remember what happened between us."

I turn as he explains further, his head bowed as he stares down as his feet. "I'm haunted by it. How you felt in my arms. What you tasted like. The curve of your waist as I held you down and lost myself in you. What you sounded like when you moaned."

My breath catches in a gasp and his head snaps up, our eyes colliding.

"Yeah, it was something like that." He nods, stepping slowly toward me.

"Luc." I breath, not entirely sure if I want him to keep coming or stop.

"My name-" He prowls closer, "on your lips." He narrows his eyes, as he drags a hand down his chin. "I've dreamed of hearing you say it again and again."

I take several steps back to counter his forward ones, my heart fluttering like a hummingbird's wings, my chest rising and falling rapidly. I hold a hand out in front of me to stop him, but he doesn't reach it, both of us freezing when a voice sounds over the monitor.

"Mama."

Luc arches a brow, a wicked smirk appearing. "Saved by the baby?"

I laugh nervously, knowing my cheeks are flushed by the heat I feel in them. "I think so."

"Let me go get her." He offers, and I nod, needing a few minutes to recover from what just happened.

What in the hell would being on the road with him be like? Stuck on a bus together. For hours at a time. Was I actually considering this? And was I doing this for Larkin or for me? Because holy hell, I'm quite sure I would have let him throw me up on the counter if he had come any closer.

This man was pure sex on a stick. Danger should be stamped on his forehead in bright red letters. He's the reason "unholy" is a category on playlists. There's sex appeal, and then there's Luc, the kind of man born entirely of chaos and bad decisions.

I needed to make sure I would be able to make good decisions when it came to my daughter. And that did not include how amazing I know he would feel on top of me.

"I think she might need a new diaper." He's holding Larkin under the armpits, both of his arms extended. He looks like he's holding a bomb that might explode and has no idea what to do with it.

Larkin's little legs dangle, toes tapping air, her eyes big and round with interest, not fear. She's perfectly calm. He is not. His brow is pulled tight as he keeps repeating, "it's okay, it's going to be okay."

Her tiny fist curls around one of his thumbs, and that's

when he freezes. Doesn't pull her closer, doesn't pull away. Just… pauses. Like he's been manually unplugged.

I watch, caught between utter amusement and fascination. And I can't help it. I smile. Not at the awkwardness, but at the care. The way he's hyper-focused, hyper gentle. As if she is made of spun glass and silk.

He has no idea that it's the single most endearing, disarming thing he's done so far. He also has no idea that I just decided we're going on tour with him.

"I'm sorry, I don't think I heard that correctly." Briana cocks her head, wide eyes gawking at me from across the table. "Larkin's father is Lucifer Sarris? From Devil's Halo? *My* Devil's Halo? The band I love and you hate?"

"Uh-huh." I nod, taking a fortifying gulp of the wine in my glass. "Yep. One in the same."

"This is a joke, right?" Her hand slams down against the wood, not in anger, but in disbelief, her mouth hanging open.

"Nope." I take another swig. "And guess what?"

"Oh, I can't even imagine what." Her response snarky.

"He wants me and Larkin to go on tour with him so he can get to know us better." The words rush out because this, I know, is going to push her over the edge.

"I need something stronger." She gets up and heads straight to the cabinet she knows I keep the hard stuff in. She grabs the bottle of Patron, two shot glasses off the shelf and plops back into her seat, brows drawn tight.

I watch as she pops the cork off the bottle and sloshes clear liquid into the short glasses. She doesn't wait for me, she grabs one and tosses the tequila in one swallow, pouring another immediately.

Her eyes snap up to mine. "I need to know everything."

So, I tell her. How Luc and I ran into each other at Sapphire Resort when I was working. How I knew almost in an instant he was Larkin's dad; the eyes a dead giveaway. I share everything he told me about our time together, how Larkin came to be. How we supposedly wanted to try and keep seeing each other.

How I was the reason he bottomed out at the end of his last tour. How their album, Ashes & Echoes is apparently all about me. Him meeting Larkin, and finally asking me to go on tour with me.

"Holy shit, girl." She swigs another shot. "This is something that would happen to me, not you."

"You'd think, right?" I huff out with a shake of my head, then lower my voice to a near whisper. "I don't know what I should do. I think I'm going to go. Do I do it?"

"Lil, if you don't get on that tour bus with him, I'm going in your place." She points a finger at me, her expression stern. "You've wondered for over a year who her dad is. You finally know. You owe it to yourself to see where this goes." She lowers her hand, mumbling sulkily as she does. "And you owe it to me. I want to go on tour."

I laugh, because it's so like Briana. The wild child who doesn't want to grow up.

"He kissed me today." I blurt out, needing so badly to share what I'm feeling with someone.

Her mouth quirks up in a smirk. "And?"

"It was literally five seconds long and I think my panties melted." I sigh, hiding my face in my hands as I feel my cheeks heat.

"I mean, Lil, he's the kind of guy who would fuck you stupid and then you'd thank him for the brain damage."

"Bri!" I cry out, coughing as I almost choke on the sip of wine I was taking.

"I'm just saying." She practically snorts. "Don't go thinking you aren't going to have sex with him. You know you will."

"I'm not some kind of slut who's going to jump into bed with him after one kiss." I defend.

"Didn't you though?" She teases, another smirk on her lips as she challenges me.

"Ugh!" I groan out. "I hate when you're right!"

"Guess I should help you pack?" She giggles, the tequila definitely hitting her.

Chapter 22
Luc

The Adventure
Angels & Airways

"I want to hold her." Mikey announces as he reaches out in an attempt to take Larkin from me. "I am her uncle after all."

"You're a depraved lunatic and there's no way I'm letting you hold my daughter." I twist my frame from Mikey's outstretched hands, moving a few feet away from him at the same time.

"Come on, dude. I'm not going to hurt her for fuck's sake." Mikey whines, arms lowering as he approaches again, this time crouching down to Larkin's level.

"Jesus, man! You can't use language like that around her!" I admonish, using a hand to gently press her head against my chest to try and cover her ears.

Mikey completely ignores the scolding, instead choosing to focus on Larkin. "Don't you want to come to your Uncle Mikey? You look just like your daddy, poor thing. Maybe you'll outgrow that and look like your mom instead."

He's cooing. Actually cooing to her in a little voice that has me wondering what alien has invaded my brother's body. He rises to his full height, which is still two inches shorter than me, and pleads again.

"I'm not going to drop her." He extends his hands again. "Just let me hold her. She's adorable."

Maybe it's from being dumbfounded into shock, but I relent and transfer her into Mikey's eager hold. "Be careful with her. She's little."

"I got her." He says and then focuses all his attention on the angel in his arms, cooing voice back in action. "Don't I Little-Kins? Uncle Mikey would never drop such a pretty baby. Especially one that's my niece. You and Uncle Mikey are gonna be thick as thieves."

To my absolute shock, Larkin's entire face lights up, the dimple in her cheek making an appearance, her tiny hands clapping in delight as she beams at my brother. My absolute, pain-in-the-ass, perpetual thorn in my side, dick of a little brother seems to have won my daughter over in less than a minute.

"Miwey!" She chirps out. Not quite Mikey, but said with so much baby conviction we all knew what she meant. Cheeks puffed, eyes bright, proud as hell of herself. Dropped the two syllables like it was a divine revelation.

My insides turn glacial. This baby, who still hasn't gifted me with a single "Dada", or even a pity "Da", just joyfully christened my brother after one smile. You could see the actual joy flash in Mikey's eyes.

I turn my head slowly toward Lily, expecting a look of horror on her face. One that should match the betrayal, the violence, the paperwork to disown my brother being filed internally. Instead, she's attempting to muffle laughter behind a hand covering her mouth, practically convulsing while doing so.

Larkin just continues to beam, seemingly delighted by the chaos she has unknowingly wrought.

"Give her back." I demand, slipping my fingers under her armpits to try and reclaim her. Mikey dips his body, pivoting to the left, tightening his hold on Larkin.

"No." He swings his gaze around to me. "You're just mad she likes me better."

"Boys." Lily is standing between us before I even have a chance to blink. "She is not a toy." She reaches out and tugs the baby from Mikey's arms into her own. "When you both learn to behave like adults, we can try this again."

"Couple of bitches is what you two are." Dean mutters from a nearby couch, taking our show in from the sidelines. "Letting some baby pussy whip you."

"Hey, that's my daughter you're talking about." I kick his sneakered foot with my booted one. "Don't be an asshole."

"Language!" Mikey chastises, pointing to Larkin. *Is he for fucking real?*

Dean rises, shaking his head. "I'm going to my room. I'll catch you for soundcheck."

"Take him with you." I order, jerking my chin toward Mikey.

"I'm going, I'm going." Mikey declares, following behind Dean, flashing a smile to Larkin as he walks by her. "See ya later, Little-kins."

"Did your brother give my baby a nick-name?" Lily ponders out loud, looking from me to the closing door.

"I don't know what in the hell that was." My brow furrowed as I respond. "Or who. I ain't ever seen my brother act like that."

Lily, Larkin and I arrived in L.A. a little over an hour ago on a private jet that Cherry had arranged for us. There was no way we were ready to announce to the world that I had a baby, let alone that she and her mother were on tour with us. Taking the jet kept things under wraps, and made the trip much easier for the three of us.

We were staying in a hotel for the next two nights while we were here. Cherry had gotten us a two-bedroom suite so Lily and Larkin could have their own space, but also enabled me to be with them.

She had also somehow managed to find an additional bus for us to use for the rest of the tour, if we needed it that long. Or, if things didn't go well, I guess one week.

It was in San Francisco though, which was our next tour stop, so we'd have to jet it there, where we could finally get settled in and hopefully get into a routine. I was counting on Lily staying for more than a week.

With the amount of stuff she had packed for Larkin, it sure seemed like she would be staying awhile. She had a car seat, a portable crib, a high chair, a stroller, some bouncy chair thing, endless amounts of clothes and blankets and diapers and toys. Don't even get me started on the bottles, the sippy cups, tiny bowls and silverware. I had no idea how much crap a baby needed.

She wanted to bring the cat too, but I had to squash that. At least until we were on the bus, then maybe we could see if it was possible. Until then, Teddy was staying with Briana.

"Well, it went much better than I expected." She's got Larkin on her jutted hip, exhaustion written all over her.

"Dean was kind of a dick." I frown. "Wasn't expecting that from him. He's usually the receptive one."

"It's a shock, Luc." She defends, smoothing a hand over

Larkin's unruly curls. "I'm sure the last thing they want is a baby on tour with them, cramping their style."

"They have their own space." I counter. "They can still do whatever the hell they want."

"I'm Yoko." She shrugs, like it should be so obvious to me.

I chuckle. "You're the furthest thing from Yoko."

I stride over. "Give her to me. You look beat. Why don't you go take a nap?"

"I was up until after three packing." She explains with a small chuckle. "And I may have had a little too much to drink with Bri."

"Go then." I wave her away. "I got this."

"You sure?" Concern in the look she's giving me. "Will you be okay if she needs to be changed or gets fussy?"

"I'm sure I can figure it out. I'm a grown-ass man." I point toward her bedroom door. "Go. Rest." I beam down at the little girl in my arms. "Nothing I want more than to spend some time with this one."

"Okay." She relents, slowly retreating away from us. "But wake me if-"

"We'll be fine." I assure her a final time, my voice more convincing than the beating of my heart pounding against my ribs. She shuts the door softly after a final glance in our direction.

"Now what, Little One?" I peer down and ask, a gummy smile the response I get. "Want to play?"

I kneel down on the floor and sit her in front of giant block that has a million different types of activities for her to explore. She pulls herself up almost instantly, and I rear back, surprised she can stand. I realize I have so many things to learn about her, about what she can and can't do, about what it means to be her dad.

I still haven't told my parents, and I know I need to. I know they'll be thrilled. But, I also know that as soon as I tell them, they'll be on the first plane out here. Not ready for that yet. I need to get a better grip on the whole fatherhood thing before I drag them into this.

Larkin plays with beads that are on a track, sliding them back and forth, her face lighting up when they drop and glide on their own. This keeps her entertained for a full ten minutes, so I transfer her to the big boppy chair thing. She bounces in it and spins around in circles, slapping at the different toys sitting on the tray around the circumference.

I marvel at the different sounds she makes. Her voice is a bit raspy, even though it's a higher pitch, and I wonder if she'll sound like me. Will she be able to sing like me? How is it possible that less than a week ago, I didn't even know a tiny version of me existed? And even more surprising, that I'm okay with it.

When she starts to get bored in the chair, I snag her up and get cozy with her on the sofa. I find some baby music on YouTube, which she seems to like, her attention mesmerized by the characters and the songs they sing. I feel her body relax into mine, and I let out a sigh of relief. She's getting more comfortable with me, and I think me with her.

"Hey you two." A hand shaking my shoulder gently has me prying my eyes open.

I jerk awake, my arms automatically tightening around Larkin, making sure she's still there. "Sorry!" I sit up straighter, heart racing. "I didn't mean to fall asleep."

"Luc." Her voice soft. "You didn't do anything wrong." She dips her chin to the precious bundle in my arms. "Look, she's totally fine."

And she is. She's sound asleep against my chest, her lips

puckered around her thumb, content and safe. This might only be the second time in my life I've woken up with a girl in my arms and liked it.

"Looks like we all needed a nap." A yawn escaping as she smiles down at us. "Want me to take her?"

"What time is it?" I scooch forward, sitting up straighter, transferring Larkin into her mother's welcome arms.

"A little after four." She informs me, her gaze locked on her daughter.

"Shit." I rise, scraping a hand down my face as I try and wake up. "I have to go to sound check."

"Go." Her hips sway slightly, Lily still sleeping like an angel. "I'm good."

I start to stride away, then stop, turning to look at the two girls that are now a permanent part of my life. "This is going to work."

Her lips turn up in a small smile. "It's not even been a day, Luc."

I shake off her reality check, restating what I know in my heart to be true. "This is going to work."

I don't wait for her to respond. I don't need her to respond. It's what I believe and because of that, I'll do every-thing in my power to make sure it does.

Little did I know, life always seems to have the final say.

Chapter 23
Lily

Electric Love
Borns

I DECIDE it's better to keep a low profile until things are more clearly defined between Luc and I, and don't go to either of his shows in Los Angeles. I could tell he was a little disappointed, but I don't have anyone to stay with Larkin and I was most definitely not bringing her to a concert at less than a year old.

He offered to let me bring my mother or even Briana with me on the tour, so I could have help with Larkin. Briana is a definite no. She's the one that would need a babysitter and I'm not up for that role. And while I know my mother would be an amazing help, and has the time, I'm not sure I want her here, witness to my grappling confusion.

There's so much more going on than Luc getting to know his child - there's the question of us. If there is even an us. It's more than obvious to me what he wants. He made it clear during his plea with me to come on this tour. And the tension that crackles between us every single time we're together is undeniable.

That one quick kiss from him had set me on fire. Heat had been simmering in my veins since, and it was probably just a matter of time before the flame between us ignited again.

I want him. I won't deny it. But would it just add a complication to his relationship with Larkin if the spark between us is just temporary? Was it merely lust and the memory, his memory anyway, of what had happened between us two years ago?

These were the endless questions that keep me tossing and turning long after Larkin had fallen asleep in her crib. Giving up on the possibility of getting any rest, I toss the covers off of me and rise from the bed.

I tiptoe over to the crib, Larkin's little body spread eagle as she snores softly. I press a kiss against my fingertips and brush them softly on her forehead.

I pad in my bare feet to the door, turning the knob before sneaking out of the room as silently as I can. I turn, my heart almost flatlining when I spy Luc sprawled lazily on one of the couches, a bottle of beer in one hand.

He's wearing a faded pair of jeans. That's all. And Christ on a cracker, he looks damn good. Who knew he had all that going on? He's lean, but his chest and abs are defined. The denim waist of his pants rests low on his hips, exposing a chiseled V that points right to his happy place. His hair is tousled and damp. Whether it's because he's sweating or just got out of the shower, I'm not sure from this far away.

He's staring at me, and I realize it's probably because I'm not wearing much either; an oversized t-shirt that does fall to mid-thigh, but no bra underneath. I glance down to see if the girls are betraying me, and of course they are at full attention, two peaks straining against the thin cotton material. I feel my cheeks heat as I dare to lift my gaze back toward Luc.

"I couldn't sleep." I stammer, frozen in place.

"Me either." He shifts so he's sitting up straight, lifting the bottle in his hand. "You want a beer?"

"Uh, sure." I nod, forcing my feet to move as I shuffle toward the couch. He rises at the same time, and I have to stop short so I don't collide with him. I tilt my head back, our eyes locking, his tongue dragging across his lower lip leaving it glistening.

"See something you like, Kitten?" His voice gravely as he stares down at me, a soft chuckle escaping those lips.

Am I panting? I feel like my chest is heaving…

"Take this one." He drawls, my attention focused entirely on his mouth as he hands me his beer. "I just opened it."

Somehow my mind has enough sense to slide my hand around the bottle, sparks tingling up my arm as our fingers brush together. He moves to his right just as I step to my left and our bodies meet in a soft collision.

I go to take a quick step back, an apology already streaming from me, but his hand wraps around the back of my neck keeping me in place. He crooks a knuckle under my chin using it to tilt it up until I can see him peering down at me.

"You're fire." He growls softly, forehead pressing to mine. "And I've spent two years pretending I'm not built to burn." His thumb traces my lip and its slow torture.

I'm silent, our breaths the only thing between us.

"I'm going to kiss you now, Lily." He rasps as his stare

penetrates through me. "I'm only warning you because if you don't want me to, you better stop me before I start."

I blink in response, feeling myself surrender as he begins to lean.

"Final warning." He murmurs, the last thing I comprehend before his lips crash against mine. His mouth possesses me like he's spent every sleepless night trying not to do this and finally snapped.

There's no polite testing of the waters. It's heat and hunger and a low, rough sound rumbling in his chest like he's starving and I'm the first real thing he's tasted in months.

The beer bottle slips from my fingers, thudding softly onto the carpet, my fingers suddenly weaving through his hair, pulling him closer, like my body decided for me that distance is no longer an option.

His lips are warm and firm and just a little desperate, and the way he kisses me - God, it's like he's pouring every unspoken thing between us into my mouth. It's messy, breathless, all teeth, grazing lips, low groans and the faint taste of hops and heat.

He tastes like danger; a little reckless, a little unholy, like sin dressed up as salvation. I stop pretending I don't want him, even knowing I might not ever recover from a man like him.

My legs find the edge of the couch, barely a brush, but it anchors me as everything inside me catches fire. His thumb strokes the side of my neck without thought, tender against the wildness of his mouth, like he can't decide whether to worship or ruin me, so he does both.

I open to him without meaning to, a soft sound escaping me. Embarrassment, longing, surrender, I don't know anymore. His answering exhale ghosts across my cheek, shaky and a little broken, like maybe he didn't expect this to feel like being handed back half of himself.

His forehead presses to mine for half a heartbeat, breath mingling, both of us trembling like the air between us could shatter.

"I tried to forget you," he murmurs. "But there isn't a world I want to be in if I can't have you." His fingers tilt my chin. "Even if it destroys me."

And then he dives back in. Deeper, slower this time, like now that he has me, he's determined to savor every second of the fall.

I should pull back. I should breathe. I should think.

But thought is impossible when his mouth is on mine, his hand in my hair, his body heat rolling off him like sin and salvation combined. And in this moment, in this dim, quiet room with only the sound of our breathing and our hearts losing their rhythm, the only truth I know is that I don't want him to stop.

Not now. *Maybe not ever.*

He pulls back only a breath, lips still brushing mine, like he's not quite ready to let go of the air between us. His forehead rests against mine, his breathing uneven, chest rising and falling like he just ran a marathon instead of kissing me senseless.

His fingers stay tangled in my hair, holding me there, not trapping, *but anchoring.* Like if he lets go, he might lose me all over again.

His voice comes low, rough, scraped raw. The sound of someone who's been holding too much in for too long. "Tell me you don't feel that?"

Not a command. Not a demand. A quiet, desperate plea.

And God help me, I do. I feel it everywhere; in my pulse, in the tremble in my knees, in the way my heart is trying to claw its way out of my chest and into his hand.

My palm settles over his heart like my body decided before my brain could argue. His breath catches, not big or dramatic, just a sharp inhale like I've reached inside his ribs without meaning to.

"I don't have the memories, Luc," I whisper, voice thin but honest. "But something in me knows you. And that scares the hell out of me."

His hand at the back of my neck tightens just slightly, thumb brushing my pulse like he can soothe panic, and claim me in the same touch. His forehead dips to mine, lips ghosting mine without pressing in, like he's savoring the proximity, like pulling away would be impossible now.

A low sound leaves him. It's not a laugh, not a breath. Something deeper. Something wrecked. Something sure.

"Yeah," he murmurs, voice rough and so achingly gentle it breaks and mends me in the same second. "I know it does." His thumb drags along my jaw, slow, deliberate, reverent. "But, let me remind you how well I know you."

Not a question. Not permission. A promise. A beginning.

His lips brush mine again, softer this time, like he's testing the edge of what we just shattered open. The kiss deepens before I even register moving, heat rushing through me so fast I swear I feel it down to my toes. He tastes like midnight, and want, and something dangerously close to home.

I don't mean to make a sound, but a quiet, helpless whimper escapes me, and everything inside him seems to snap. His hand slides from my neck to my waist, fingers splaying against bare skin where my shirt has ridden up. The touch scorches. It steals my breath, my thoughts, every shred of sense I might've had left.

He tugs me just enough that his body is crowding mine, warmth and muscle and barely restrained hunger. My knees go weak. My fingers curl into his hair, holding on because if I let go, I think gravity would just take me down and leave me in pieces at his feet.

His chest rises and falls hard against mine, each breath rough and uneven. And when his mouth leaves mine for a second, dragging slow across my cheek to my jaw, I feel the world tilt.

God, I want him. And I don't even know why. I just *do.* In my bones. In my blood. He nips lightly at my bottom lip before kissing me again, deeper, slower, like he's trying to memorize the shape of my soul through our mouths.

My body arches toward him without permission, need sparking hot under my skin straight to my core, and that's when panic hits. Not because he's too close. But because it feels *too right.* Too familiar for someone I don't remember.

I break the kiss, breath tearing out of me, palms flat against his chest like I'm bracing for impact. His heart pounds under my hand, strong and heavy, and it only makes the ache worse.

"I-" My voice stumbles, barely there as I shake my head, my hair swishing around my face. "I don't think... I'm not ready."

His eyes close like he's holding back something sharp; a groan, a curse, maybe both. When he opens them again, they're softer. Wrecked and steady at the same time. He lifts one hand, his thumb brushing the corner of my mouth where his kiss still burns.

"It's okay." His voice is smoke and gravel, low and

unbearably gentle. Then, quiet enough to sting, "I'm not rushing this. Not again. You may not remember us, but I do, and I'll wait for you to want me with your heart, not just your body."

He leans his forehead to mine for a beat, one last touch, one last breath shared as he makes me a final promise. "Because, trust me Lily, when we get there, you'll know. You'll feel every damn second of it."

He takes several steps away, jaw tight like the act costs him every last bit of reserve he has left. And God help me, the space between us feels colder than the night air.

Chapter 24
Luc

More Than Words
Extreme

To say being on the road with a baby, and a woman I hope to sometime soon call my own, strange, would be an understatement. It is a complete and utter mind fuck. This isn't to say things are bad. They aren't. This is actually going incredibly well, all things considered.

I went from being a very single, very detached man, to one who is currently holding a baby in his lap, attempting to read a book to her. Happily, I might add. The woman of my dreams sitting a foot away. And, all of this change happened just over a week ago.

We finished our set in San Francisco last night, and we are on our way to Portland now. Our crew guys had moved everything from our room onto the bus, and Lily had spent most of yesterday getting everything organized for Larkin.

It was a damn nice bus. Brand new from what I could tell.

Cherry must have had a hell of time convincing the label we needed it and why. If it meant a cut out of my tour royalties, it would be well worth it.

The main cabin looked like a big open concept living space. One side was lined with a kitchen, complete with a full-size fridge, stove, microwave, plenty of cabinets, with fancy granite countertops to boot. At the end of the wall, a huge flat screen was mounted above a gas fireplace. Not sure we'd need that during the summer, but it was a nice touch.

The other side of the bus had a long, velvet covered sofa, and a dining table with two bench seats. The bedroom was on the backside of the bus, separated by a sliding door. It only had a queen size bed, but the smaller sized bed allowed for more floor space, and a place to setup Larkin's temporary crib.

The bathroom was off the bedroom, and rivaled most of the hotel bathrooms I'd had over the years. The only problem we encountered was a bathtub. There wasn't one. Lily promised she could manage, either bathing Larkin in the large kitchen sink, or just taking her into the shower with her.

Okay, maybe that wasn't the only problem. The other one, the single bedroom, was the other, and our current topic of conversation.

"Lily, I've got no problem at all sleeping right here." I point to the couch I'm sitting on. "It folds down, and is plenty long enough."

"It feels wrong." She argues back. "You're the one on tour, going out on stage every night. You need to make sure you're getting the rest that you need."

"Believe me, I've slept in places a hundred times worse than this couch." I fire back with a chuckle. "This isn't a hardship." I lower my voice as I point to a picture in the book I'm holding in front of Larkin. "What's this called?"

"Cat." She blurts out, Lily and I clapping our hands in delight, our other subject momentarily put aside.

"Good girl!" I exclaim, kissing the top of her head. "You're so smart." I turn my attention back to Lily, arching a brow suggestively. "I could always just sleep in the bed with you."

Her face flushes a deep pink, her eyes popping wide as she shifts her gaze down to the bundle in my lap. I'm quite sure Larkin doesn't have a clue what I'm referencing.

Since our heated moment in Los Angeles the other night, I've been biding my time, giving her the space she asked for while we get to know each other, more properly than our original meeting. But it isn't easy.

Just looking at her made my cock twitch. I wanted another taste of her more than I wanted my next breath. I didn't want to scare her away though, so I wait. Not without a subtle hint every now and then though, like the one I just planted, to make sure she knows I want her. That won't, and isn't going to change.

There's been one other moment since that night in L.A., even hotter than the first, which happened last night after the show when I got back to our room. I was a sweaty mess. She was freshly showered, sitting in a chair, brushing her long hair, the wet ends dripping onto her shirt, making it basically transparent. She may as well have been naked.

I'm a patient man, but I'm also human. And after a show, I'm already fucking edgy as hell, my endorphins so high I usually need a good couple of hours to come down. I couldn't help myself. I prowled straight to her, sank down beside her, then yanked her onto my lap as I crushed my mouth to hers.

There wasn't a single second of hesitation on her part. In minutes, she had readjusted herself so her legs straddled my waist, her center lining up perfectly against my cock. The fucking heat that came from between her legs, even through the jeans I had on, was like hell on earth. I wanted to bury myself so deep inside her, hear her scream my name again, feel her wrap around me like a vise.

But she had to be the one to make that happen. And until she gave me the okay, my poor cock would keep having regular visits with my palm in the shower. I'm surprised I don't have blisters yet. And maybe it would have happened last night, but Larkin woke up crying, Lily's heat, scent, body, gone before I could even register the loss.

I turn the page, literally and figuratively, and focus on the little nugget in my lap. She seems to be completely at ease with me, even reaching out for me now when I enter the room.

I never knew I could love something so much. Of course, every time Mikey's around, I become invisible. Never in a million years did I think my brother would win over a girl, let alone, the one I love the most. Sometimes the universe has a sick sense of humor.

"I just want to remind you that the reporter from Amped will be joining us on tour starting in Portland."

This has been a thorn in my side from the moment I had learned about it, but it pricked even harder now that Lily and Larkin were in my life.

"Cherry's making her sign an NDA specific to you and Larkin. She's got full access to the band, including me, but you two are off limits."

"Do you think she'll actually abide by that?" Her brow furrowing. "She's a reporter. Isn't this the kind of thing they live for." She chuffs. "Whoever breaks the story about your little love child will be hitting paydirt."

"Cherry's the best." I reassure her, lowering a wiggling Larkin to the floor so she can crawl around. "We have kick-ass lawyers. She wouldn't allow something that she thinks would harm the band or any of us in it."

"Okay." She sighs, getting up to redirect Larkin away from a cabinet in the kitchen. "If you trust her, then I have too as well."

"This chick did a number on me when I crashed and burned last tour." The confession, one that doesn't come easily due to the nature of its occurrence. "When I thought you had ghosted me, and I went a little too wild-child."

"So why is Cherry letting her go on tour with the band then?" General concern in her tone.

"Four grammy's and album of the year." I scoff with a shrug. "We're the biggest rock band in the world right now. We need to redeem ourselves to the magazine and their following, and apparently this is how we do it."

"Personally, I think it sucks." A hand on her hip as she expresses her opinion.

I throw my head back as I laugh, loving that she's on the same page as me. "We'll make it work. I'm not going to let anyone near you or Larkin."

She lowers her body to sit cross-legged on the floor to play with Larkin. She's a really good mom. I know I've only seen her in action for a week, but it's so obvious in how she is with her. I watch them as they interact, my heart growing fuller than I could have ever dreamed, and I know that I will do anything to keep them safe.

"I'm falling in love with you." It's out there before I even realize I've said it out loud, her head whipping up, her eyes locking onto mine.

"Luc." Her response a mere whisper as a hand covers her mouth.

"I don't expect you to say it back." I rush out, leaning forward, resting my elbows on my knees as I place my hands under my chin. "I just want you to know that this isn't something trivial for me. It's real. More fucking real than anything I've ever felt before."

She blinks several times, and I realize it's because tears are brimming in her eyes. She looks down, brushing them away before they can fall.

"Shit." I drop down onto my knees on the floor to get closer to her. "I'm sorry. I shouldn't have said anything."

She shakes her head, then looks over at me, the corners of her mouth lifting slightly. "I'm happy, Luc, not sad." She sniffles, handing a toy to Larkin before continuing.

"I wondered so many times who Larkin's father was. Hated that I couldn't remember. Hated that I didn't know if I would ever find out." She lets out a small chuckle. "And now that I know-" She breathes out a long sigh. "I'm so relieved. You could have been anyone. I mean, I didn't expect her dad to be a famous rockstar, that's for sure." She laughs again. "You're kind. And you care. And you want the best for her, for us."

"But-" I urge, because I can feel it coming.

"You're a rockstar. You're famous. You have this reputation for being a player." She winces as she explains. "I may have googled you."

"That was before you. Before I knew about Larkin." I defend the later, knowing I can't do anything about the famous rockstar part.

"I know, I know." She frowns. "Luc, your gorgeous. Like, really, really hot as hell kind of good looking." She waves a hand up and down the length of my body. "How could I not want you? I think it's pretty obvious in case you couldn't tell after the last few times you kissed me."

She glances down at Larkin, who's playing with some blocks, then hisses out. "If she wasn't here right now, I'd be climbing you like a tree."

"So, what's the problem then?" I urge, because there's a reason she's holding back but I don't understand what it is.

"That is the problem." She declares, like it should be obvious.

"I don't understand." My head tilting in confusion.

"Luc, I need to know my feelings for you aren't going to be based on how I'm going to feel by F-U-C-K-I-N-G you. Because, I have no doubt it would be amazing."

She actually spells the word out. Which makes me chuckle, even though this is a serious conversation and one we need to have.

"I can tell you from past experience that it will be." I grumble, not because I'm angry, but because I know what she's saying is true. I have two years of unrequited memories that tell me what I feel for her is more than lust. Two years that she doesn't have privy to because of her accident.

I scoot closer to her and take her hand in mine. "I didn't say the words to scare you or rush you. Take all the time you need. Just know, I'm in it. One thousand percent. If that's what you decide you want from me."

"Thank you." She breathes, squeezing her fingers in mine.

"To be clear though, I'm completely fine if you just want to use my really, really hot body and climb me like a tree." I quirk a devilish smile at her.

"The temptation to accept that offer is getting harder and harder to ignore." She admits, a sheepish look on her face as she blushes.

What she doesn't know, and what I keep to myself, is I don't need her consent to claim what I know is already mine.

It's written in the stars. It's just a matter of when.

Chapter 25
Lily

Breathe
Anna Nalick

I SPEND the rest of the next day convincing myself I can do this. That leaving Larkin with Rita, our bus driver, for a few hours won't spontaneously combust the universe. She's sound asleep, and Rita has been part of Luc's road crew for years.

The reasonable part of my brain knows I need air, time away for myself. The irrational part keeps whispering *bad idea, abort mission, take the baby and run.*

But when I looked at Luc earlier, stretched out across the couch, guitar resting against his thigh, sunlight leaking over his bare chest, the fear softened. I knew I could do this. I *wanted* to see him in his world. I wanted to see him onstage.

Which is how I find myself at the venue door, breathing like I just ran a marathon I didn't train for.

"You sure?" Luc asks gently. Not doubtful, just making sure I have an exit if I need one.

"I'm sure," I lie. My voice sounds two seconds from hysterical laughter, but whatever. We're here. We're doing this.

He smirks like he knows I'm panicking and finds it adorable. Annoying man. Inside, it's chaos; the buzzing, frantic kind. Crew weaving through corridors, radios crackling, amps rumbling through walls. It's alive, electric, and... loud.

A security guard steps in front of us with a clipboard and a stack of stapled packets. "She needs to sign before she can go any further." Luc stiffens beside me.

The top page reads:

Non-Disclosure and Confidentiality Agreement
Pertaining to the private lives of Lucifer Sarris and minor child known as...

"You have a kid?" The guard blurts, blinking over at Luc before I can even inhale. Luc takes one step forward with predatory calm, his voice quiet and lethal. "Say another word and I swear to-"

"Got it, got it," the guy stammers, thrusting a pen at me like a peace offering.

My throat tightens as I sign. It's not the NDA. It's the reminder. Being here puts a target on my child. On *us*.

Luc brushes his thumb over the back of my hand when I hand the papers back. "This is just protection," he murmurs. "Not restriction. Not for you."

Somehow, that helps. Somehow, it also makes my stomach flip like it's auditioning for gymnastics nationals.

We move deeper into the venue, and the first crack hits, splintering my false sense of security. The hallway opens near the general entrance, and suddenly we're caught in a fast-moving wave of fans shifting past barricades.

Security holds them back, but one girl screams when she recognizes Luc. "OH MY GOD—LUC! LOOOOVE YOU!" Another girl shoves in her excitement, bumping my shoulder. Hard.

"Watch it!" Someone yells, definitely not me, but I think it loudly enough.

A guy behind me mutters, "Looks like Luc got himself another backstage toy."

My spine snaps straight. Heat shoots through me as anger, humiliation, and protective rage I didn't know I could produce surges.

Luc hears. I feel him *hear* it. A growl vibrates low in his chest, feral and dangerous, his hand tightening around mine. "It means nothing. Ignore it."

He shifts, stepping between me and the crowd, shoulders tense, gaze razor-sharp. "You okay?" he murmurs, hand sliding to my lower back. Not possessive. Protective.

"Yes," I whisper. No idea if it's true. We make it through, breath shaky, adrenaline humming. And that's when I see her. Different than I thought, but recognizable by the press badge she's got clipped to her camera strap.

She's wearing cut-off jean shorts, a dark t-shirt that's seen better days, and black combat boots. Her brown hair is piled on top of her head in a messy bun, and a Nikon hangs from her neck. She's younger than I expected, maybe in her late twenties. But it's her eyes I notice. Eyes that say she's already unimpressed with this world.

Dean's there, leaning against a road case, arms crossed, smirk already locked and loaded, staring her down like she's a challenge he wants to unwrap.

"I don't do fluff pieces," she's saying as we approach.

Dean snorts. "Relax, sweetheart. Nobody asked you to."

A single brow arches. "Sweetheart?"

I don't know her yet, but I think I already love her. And also, maybe slightly fear her.

"You journalists always show up acting like you're saving rock 'n' roll," Dean drawls. "Pretty sure we've been doing just fine without your moral compass."

"Oh, don't worry," she shoots back, voice like ice that could scald. "I don't plan to waste any time on morality here."

Dean blinks. Then grins like she just handed him a dare.

Luc leans down, lips brushing my ear. "Incoming hurricane."

"Dean or her?" I whisper.

"Both."

Luc is called over to gear up. He touches my hip, looks into my eyes for one beat longer than necessary. The kind of look that fills my lungs and steals my breath at the same time.

"Stay close," he murmurs.

I nod. Watch him go. Then let out a breath I didn't realize I was holding. My brain is cycling between *this is fine* and *what the hell am I doing here.*

Except... I *am* here. I chose to be. And for the first time today, beneath the nerves and the adrenaline and the roar of a waiting crowd, it hits me, maybe I'm allowed to belong here too. I'm here for him. And maybe, maybe I'm here for me too.

And suddenly, I realize I'm standing beside the world's most chaotic budding hate-relationship duo. The reporter is still staring Dean down like she could set him on fire with sheer will, when her gaze flicks to me. In an instant her expression shifts.

The heat is gone, steel softening, like her brain just switched files. "You must be Lily," she says, and her tone surprises me. Warm. Normal. Human. Not sharp or postured like she was two seconds ago.

I blink. "I- yeah. Hi."

Up close she's not intimidating, or, okay, she totally still is, but there's a glimmer in her eyes I recognize. She's someone who has walked into rooms full of louder voices and refused to shrink.

She extends her hand. "Sadie Brooks. I promise I don't bite." She shifts her gaze momentarily to Dean. "Unless you're a lead guitarist with a God complex."

Dean snorts. "Journalists with superiority issues are my favorite species, thanks."

I shake her hand before I can overthink it. "I'm not entirely sure what's happening right now," I admit.

Sadie smiles. A real one, not a reporter kind of fake smile. "Trust me, neither is he."

Dean opens his mouth. Probably to say something cocky and inappropriate. We both ignore him.

"You're staying on the tour?" Sadie asks, eyes flicking to my backstage pass, then to the direction Luc disappeared in.

"I- trying to," I say, honest because lying feels pointless. "If I don't have a panic attack first."

She doesn't laugh. Doesn't brush it off. She nods like she gets it, like she's had her own version of that thought every time she walked into a new arena with her notebook and her spine made of steel.

"If you need air later, come find me." She offers quietly. "I know all the good hiding spots around here."

Warmth hits my chest. Unexpected kindness. Exactly when I need it. "Thank you."

Dean scoffs. "Oh great. Girl gang forming. Let's just add it to the list of things this tour doesn't need."

Sadie gives him a dazzling smile that does not reach her eyes. "Careful, Ross. Some of us came here to observe. Not worship."

He looks personally offended. I try very hard not to laugh. Maybe I *will* survive this tour after all.

We step into the area behind the stage we've been directed to, just as lights sweep across the crowd, thousands of screaming fans already swaying to the opening band. The scale of it bowls into me. Echoes. The tang of metal and dust. The loud hum of amps. Bodies moving everywhere, purposeful and loud. Too loud.

My pulse kicks up. I tell myself it's excitement, not panic. Excitement sounds prettier. I cling to that thought for exactly three seconds.

Then all the lights slam on, flooding the arena in bright white, the warm-up band coming off the stage, a ripple of screams echoing from fans calling out for Devil's Halo. The sound slices straight down my spine.

Breathe. Why can't I breathe? Why does my chest feel like it shrunk?

Luc is halfway to the stage stairs, talking to someone. I try to focus on his voice; low, steady, familiar, but everything else swells instead. Light. Noise. Movement. Shadow. Too much space and nowhere to hide in it.

My throat goes tight. Fingers numb. Oh God. I grip the wall beside me like it's the only thing tethering me to the earth. Breathe. It's fine. You're fine. You are absolutely-

"Hey." A soft voice at my elbow. Sadie. She doesn't crowd

me. Doesn't grab me. Just angles her body so she blocks the open space, dulling the chaos behind us by an inch. Her eyes flick over my face. Sharp. Knowing. Kind in a way that hits me behind the ribs.

"Breathe," she murmurs. "I've got you."

Air shudders out of me. I suck another in. She matches pace quietly, like she's done this before; panic or stadiums or, maybe both.

My vision stops tunneling just in time for Luc to notice. His gaze snaps to me and something shifts in his posture, concern wrapped in heat with purpose and protectiveness. His feet move before the thought finishes.

He doesn't ask what's wrong. He just steps into my space, hand sliding to the back of my neck, thumb brushing the curve just below my ear. Warm. Solid. Human-sized in a world suddenly too big.

"Hey," he crouches so he's eye level with me, his voice low, steady enough to stand on. "You with me?"

I nod. A shaky, humiliating little thing, and his forehead touches mine for one heartbeat. And we take one breath together. Everything steadies. Like he flipped a switch inside me I didn't know existed.

"You're okay," He assures me. "We do this together. No rush. No pressure. Just… be here with me."

God, I could fall for him. I already am, in ways I don't have names for yet.

Sadie backs up half a step, giving space but not distance. Like she's anchoring me from the other side. A silent *I'm not going anywhere either.* And suddenly the arena doesn't feel so big. Or I don't feel so small.

Luc gives one last soft touch, his thumb brushing my jaw like a promise, just before the stage manager waves him over.

"I'll be right there," he murmurs. "If you need out, just look at me."

I nod. I don't trust my voice not to wobble.

He jogs up the stairs, and somehow the entire arena shifts around him, like gravity re-calibrates for him alone. Sound techs snap to attention. Lights adjust. And suddenly I'm watching not just Luc, but the *rockstar* Luc that the world screams for. The man with a microphone and a pulse that commands stadiums.

My heart is a traitor. It's proud. I breathe again. And then-

"What was that?" Dean's voice slices in, sharp and incredulous as he peers at Sadie. He's standing a few feet away, arms crossed like he's preparing to be offended by the world again.

Sadie lifts a brow. Calm. Unmovable. "It's called empathy, Ross. Try it sometime."

He scoffs. "He's a rockstar. She's with him. There's gonna be noise, crowds, people breathing the same air. If she can't handle it-"

Sadie's eyes narrow just a fraction, warmth gone, journalist steel sliding into place.

"If you finish that sentence, I'm going to write an entire paragraph about the fragile egos of lead guitarists."

Dean opens his mouth. Closes it. Points a finger at her instead, like that's somehow a rebuttal. "I wasn't being a dick," he mutters. "I was just saying."

"Stop saying." Sadie barks back, offering him a tight, diplomatic smile that somehow feels like a threat. "It was going so well for you."

I choke on a laugh. Dean shoots me a betrayed look. Like

I've personally joined an anti-Dean rebellion. In fairness, maybe I have.

He mutters something about "journalists with savior complexes" and stalks off, grabbing a guitar from his roadie as if the instrument personally understands him better than we do.

Sadie exhales and shakes her head. "God, that man needs therapy. Or a hug. Or both, in that order."

"Probably the therapy," I manage, still catching my breath from, everything. "He'd fight the hug."

"He'd lose," she deadpans. I believe her.

Before I can respond, a ripple moves across the crew, subtle, instinctive, and the sound system hums alive. The arena hushes like something ancient just woke up.

Luc steps up to the mic. And the world narrows to him. He's not even singing yet, just standing, letting the lead in of the song play, a low hum that vibrates in my bones. He looks up, finds me, and something in his face softens then sharpens, like I'm the reason he does this and the reason he has to do it well.

Then he starts. And oh, wow. I get it now. This isn't the man who held me steady five minutes ago. This is wildfire in human form. Raw voice, scraped and beautiful, curling through the arena like smoke that seduces, instead of suffocates.

Lights catch on his skin, gold and shadow and sin, and every ounce of restraint we traded in the bus turns into a slow-burning ache low in my belly. I knew he was talented. What I didn't know, was that he could make *breathing* feel optional.

Sadie leans closer, whispering just loud enough for me to hear over the echoing chords.

"Yeah. That's the part that ruins you a little."

I swallow hard. "A little?"

She huffs a laugh. "Give it time."

Onstage, Luc hits a note that feels like it cracks something between my ribs. His eyes find mine again. He doesn't smile. Doesn't wink. He *claims*. Quiet. Unspoken. Certain.

God help me. He owns me with that one look. I may not have told him. I may not even be able to admit it to myself, but I'm already his.

Chapter 26
Luc

I BELT out the final song of our encore, and even though my throat is raw from the two hours we've been on stage, I would happily sing another hour if the arena allowed for it. I love performing, but I honestly can't wait to be back stage and near Lily again.

I witnessed a shift in the way she looked at me tonight. The way she put her trust entirely in my hands. That cranked up my desire for her to a fever pitch that had my fingers itching to touch her, have her in my grasp again.

And that's exactly what I do when I trot off stage, grabbing her around the waist with one hand, the other hooking around the back of her neck as I smash my mouth against hers. Her hands fist in my sweaty locks, pulling me closer, and I know this is it. This is the moment I've been waiting for. For her head to catch up with what her heart already knows.

"Get a fucking room." Mikey grumbles as he brushes past us, pulling me back to reality, both of us breaking apart on a laugh.

"Not gonna apologize for that." I press my forehead to hers, sweat still rolling down my back from the heat of the lights.

"Wasn't looking for one." She retorts, her light blue eyes dancing with mirth.

"Um, not to break up this little reunion, but you two might want to take this somewhere else more private." Sadie dips her chin toward a group of onlookers at the side of the stage.

"Yep." I drape an arm over Lily's shoulder and lead us in the direction of our backstage room. I nod over at the reporter, who's a couple steps behind us. "Thanks."

When we reach the doorway to the room, Lily dips out from under my hold and steps away. "I'll meet you back on the bus."

"What? Why?" My brow furrowing. "I want you to stay. We'll go back together."

She darts a glance into the room full of people, and then back at me. Mikey's got a bottle of tequila in his hand, and Dean's leaning over some barely dressed girl against the wall.

"I don't want to cramp your style." She waves a hand in the direction of the door. "Go have fun with the guys. I'll just see you later."

"Lily," my voice low, "You are all the fun I want and need." I toss a look over my shoulder toward the room. "That's just white noise."

"Those are your best friends." She contends. "I'm not having you choose between me and them."

I blow out a sigh as I roll my shoulders in an attempt to

chill myself out. "There is no choice here. Yeah, they're my best friends. Nothing is going to change that. Not me being with you. Not having you on tour with us. Not me leaving with you instead of partying with them."

I rest a hand on her shoulder and lean into her. "Whatever I do, isn't going to change what they do or how they feel about me. You understand that?"

"Why do you have to be so perfect?" She shakes her head, trying to contain a smile as her teeth chomp down onto her lower lip.

"You know that drives me fucking crazy." My eyes dart to her mouth. "I want to be the one biting that lip."

"Luc," Her voice barely a whisper.

"I'm trying to be patient, but I'm not going to lie baby. I want to fuck you more than I want to take my next breath." I cup her face and sweep my thumb over her cheek, pressing a kiss to her forehead. "A man only has so much will power, and mine's about to snap."

"I want you too." She confesses, eyes locking onto me.

We're back at the bus within ten minutes, and the second the door clicks shut behind Rita, the silence hits. Not real silence, but the kind that wraps around you and says *this moment belongs to no one but us.*

Lily's standing there in the soft lamplight, hair loose, cheeks flushed, the afterglow of adrenaline still clinging to her skin like stage dust on mine. She has no idea how beautiful she looks like this. How dangerous she is to me.

She turns, and when her eyes meet mine, something in my chest tilts off its axis. I've been on stages in front of thousands, bathed in light and noise, but nothing has ever felt as overwhelming as her in this quiet.

"Luc..."

My name from her hits harder than any crowd roar ever could. There's hesitation in her eyes, but it's not about me, but about the leap. About trusting where her heart is trying to go. I take a slow step toward her. Careful. Controlled. If I rush, I know I could ruin it.

"Tell me now if you don't want this," I say, voice low, steadying myself as much as her. "Because you know how I feel."

She breathes in, shaky. Brave. "I want this."

And just like that, every restraint I've been clinging to frays. Not snaps, but frays, soft and slow, like silk unraveling in candlelight. I reach for her face, fingers tracing her jaw, and she leans into the touch like she's been holding her breath for two years. That alone almost knocks me out. I press my forehead to hers, eyes closed for a second.

"I'm not touching you like a memory," I whisper. "I'm touching you like you're my future."

She shivers. My pulse stumbles.

When I kiss her, it's soft at first, reverent, careful, tasting the promise she's giving me. Then she makes this tiny sound in the back of her throat and my entire body tightens with it. I kiss her deeper, slower, like I have all night and all our lives. I'm going to savor every second of having her in my hands again.

We end up on the couch, her knees bracketing my hips, breath mixing with mine. She wearing a dress, very much like the one when we spent our first full day together two years ago. She hasn't said it, but I know she did it for me.

My hands find the hem of the skirt, sliding under the material, relearning the map of her skin. She looks down at me, eyes heavy with want, and that's it, every vow I ever made to take it slow, to be patient, goes up in smoke.

It's not lust. It's more than need. It's recognition. Her body remembering what her mind forgot. "Lily…" My voice breaks on her name. I don't care. She deserves honesty, not armor.

Her fingers thread into my hair, gentle and yes, claiming. "I choose this. I choose you."

Fuck me. Those words wreck me. They'll stay under my skin forever.

I tug her closer, moving with her like we've done this a thousand times and never once forgot how. No hurry, no rush, just heat and breath and the kind of connection you don't get twice in a lifetime, but yet, somehow, we managed to find it.

She lifts her arms as I peel the dress off and drop it to the floor. She's in nothing but panties, my cock straining against denim and reason. I strip my shirt, and she's already working the button on my jeans, rising to her knees so I can shove them down. She slides off to tug away my boots and jeans completely, her hair falling her face like a halo gone wrong.

We don't say a word. We don't need to. Every look, every touch that passes between us says more than any words could.

She slides her panties off, and moves to straddle me again, but I guide her back, easing her onto the couch. "Let me," I murmur.

I start at her ankle, peppering kisses up her calf, behind her knee, and then up the inside of her thigh.

She spreads her legs wider, her center glistening it's so wet, and I drag my tongue through her folds, tasting every thing I've missed. Her back arches, a whimper sounding from her; a sound that I swear I'll hear forever. Her nails dig into my scalp as my tongue moves slow, steady, then deeper, building until she's trembling under my hands. I don't stop until she comes apart, until she gasps my name like it's the only one she will ever need to say again.

I give her a moment to breathe, then crawl up her body, kissing every inch until I reach her breasts. I suck one nipple into my mouth, hard, then the other, my hands anchoring her hips when she writhes against me.

Her fingers find my shoulders, dragging, needy. I move higher, capturing her mouth, tasting her, tasting *us*. My body shakes with need, cock throbbing, slick at the tip.

I shift my hips so I'm between her legs, line myself up to her core, and push, slow, deep, inch by inch, until every nerve is me screams with relief. Her eyes flutter open, and for one long heartbeat, we just exist like that. Connected. Whole. It isn't fire, it's like loss of gravity. Warm, steady, consuming us from the inside out. Floating in a place that is entirely our own. A magnet locking into place where it always belonged.

Then I move. Not fast. Not frantic. Just a rhythm we fall into naturally, bodies remembering the choreography our minds forgot. Her hips rise to meet mine, soft gasps turning to moans, her nails scoring my back as the couch creaks in protest.

I brace my forearm beside her head, the other hand gripping her thigh, guiding her to move with me. Each slow thrust drags a new sound from her throat – half gasp, half plea, and I match each one with my breath against her ear. The rhythm builds like a song that refuses to fade. The longer we move, the more everything else blurs until there's only pulse and skin and the sound of her moaning my name.

The air grows thick with heat, our breaths, our heartbeats. My control starts to slip. She feels too good, too right. "Look at me." I whisper.

Her eyes lock on mine, glassy and full of everything I've been starving for.

"I've got you," I tell her, my voice rough. "I'm right here."

"Luc..." she breathes, hips trembling under my hold.

"Come for me, baby."

She does. Her entire body bows, tight and trembling, and I follow, because there's no universe where I don't. The pleasure rips through me, hot and consuming, every muscle pulled taut as I spill inside her, lost in the sound of her release.

The only light is the lamplight, the hum of the fridge in the background, the quiet breath of our daughter asleep down the hall.

I brush a strand of hair from Lily's cheek. She smiles, soft and wrecked and real.

We don't say a word, we don't need to. It's in the silence, in the heartbeat pressed against mine, in the way she sighs my name like a promise that's finally found its way home.

We stay tangled long after the tremors fade, hearts tripping over each other. The air tastes like salt and forgiveness. When she finally smiles, it's the slow kind that says she knows exactly what we just rebuilt.

I WAKE UP TO WARMTH. Her breath on my chest, the soft weight of her thigh over mine, her fingertips curled in the fabric of my shirt like even asleep she's afraid I'll disappear. I've never felt more whole than I do in this single, quiet second.

Then—

BANG. BANG. BANG.

The bus door shakes. A fist hammering it like the world's ending.

"LUC! GET UP! You need to see this! NOW!" Dean. And he sounds - not cocky. Not amused. Panicked.

Lily flinches awake, bolting upright, eyes wide. Larkin stirs in the bedroom behind us, a little whimper floating through the quiet before settling again.

"What?" she whispers, voice raw with sleep and leftover tenderness.

I don't have time to answer. Another slam. Harder.

"Luc! Open the damn door!"

I throw on sweats and open the door. Dean barrels inside holding his phone like it's a bomb. And then I see the screen. A photo. Grainy but unmistakable. *Lily. With Larkin in her arms. Outside the bus yesterday.*

A headline screaming across it:

ROCKSTAR LUCIFER SARRIS' SECRET BABY & MYSTERY MOTHER EXPOSED

Comments underneath including a flood of speculation, invasiveness, poison disguised as curiosity. My stomach drops. No, it *crashes.*

Behind me, Lily's breath stutters. "Oh God."

A whisper. A prayer. A wound.

I turn just as she sees the screen glow reflecting in my face. Her expression fractures. Shock first, then terror, then something worse - resolve born from fear.

"No, no, no." She's whispering to herself, already standing, already looking toward the bedroom. "We can't. We have to go. NOW."

"Lily, wait." I move toward her, hands out, slow, like she's a bird about to fly into a window. "We'll handle it. My team will bury it."

She shakes her head, arms wrapping around herself like armor. "You can't bury the internet, Luc. They know about her." Her voice breaks on *her.*

And that's when it hits home. This isn't about pride, or privacy, or me. It's a mama grizzly bear who thinks a forest fire is coming. Her only concern is Larkin.

"If we stay, she gets hurt. I won't let strangers talk about my baby. I won't let this world, your world-" Her mouth trembles. She stops herself, hating the way her voice edges toward panic.

I try again, softer. "We'll protect you both. We'll-"

"You can't protect us from *everyone.*" Her voice cracks. She moves toward the bedroom, shaking. "I have to go."

It feels like someone reaches into my chest and rips something vital out barehanded. Dean looks away with a shake of his head. This is too personal, even for him.

"Lily." I say her name like I'm trying to stop time. "Please."

"I have to protect my daughter first." She pauses, and hope flares so sharp it hurts. Then she says it. "I have to leave. This isn't just about me. It's about keeping her safe. Not letting vultures peck away at her until there's nothing left."

And God, I admire her even as it destroys me. "I know," I whisper. Because I do.

And that's the worst part. But it doesn't stop me from trying to get her to stay.

"Lily, it's been two days." I rake a hand through my hair as I plead with her. "Give me a chance to work with security, with Cherry. We can do more to make sure you and Larkin are protected."

"I'm not risking Larkin's well-being on a chance." Her mouth set in a firm line as she blinks back tears threatening to fall. "No matter how much I may want to stay for me, I'm leaving for her."

She disappears into the bedroom and thirty short minutes later comes out holding Larkin, bags half-packed and hands trembling.

I want to grab her. Beg. Promise her the world and my name and every song I'll ever write. But she's already breaking. I'm not going to shatter her more.

"I called Cherry. She's booking her a plane." Dean says quietly behind me. "Private's faster."

I don't look at him. I can't. I can only look at her.

Her eyes meet mine, devastated and determined all at once.

"I'm sorry," she whispers.

"I'm not," I say, voice barely steady. "You're doing what a mother does."

Her chin trembles. She nods once, like it's the only thing holding her together. Then she walks past me. And takes my heart with her.

The bus door shuts behind her with a soft click. And I stand there barefoot on the cold floor, staring at empty space, feeling more exposed than I ever have under lights and thousands of eyes.

Dean finally exhales. "Luc."

"Don't." My voice is hard as steel. But inside, I am on fire and drowning at the same time. And only one thought cuts through the chaos.

I am going to get them back.

Both of them.

Whatever it takes.

Chapter 27
Lily

Everlong
(Acoustic Version)
Foo Fighters

I DON'T REMEMBER GETTING off the plane.

I remember holding Larkin like someone might try to steal her the moment I blinked. I remember Briana's arms around me at the curb, the smell of her vanilla shampoo, the way she pulled me in like she could glue the pieces back together by sheer force of love. I remember my voice shaking when I whispered, "Everyone knows, Bri. Everyone."

I don't remember the drive.

But I remember the silence that followed. Even laughter at Bri's house feels wrong, like I'm trespassing in a life I thought I wanted, normal, quiet, safe. Only now it feels like hiding. Like being safe is suddenly the most dangerous thing of all. Even Teddy seems to know something is wrong, hiding in Bri's bedroom instead of planting himself in my lap.

Larkin babbles on the floor in her little bouncy seat, oblivious and happy, and I swear if I stare at her too long, I'll either fall apart completely or become stone. Maybe both. Looking at her is a reminder of the beautiful man that helped to create her.

"I'm doing the right thing," I whisper trying to convince myself. Because I *have to believe that.* Don't I?

Except Bri doesn't buy it for a second. She slides a mug of tea toward me and sits, eyes soft but unyielding. "You left because you're a mom. Good. That's what good moms do." She pauses. "But are you really protecting her right now? Or are you protecting yourself from being hurt again?"

The question hits like cold water poured down my spine. I open my mouth to argue, then snap it shut. I am protecting her, but the words don't feel right when I try to say them. They taste like fear.

Bri squeezes my hand. "You fell in love with him." It's not a question. It's a mirror.

I swallow hard. "I didn't want to. I didn't plan to."

"Yeah, well," she shrugs, her lips tilting up into a soft smile. "Love rarely fills out the appropriate paperwork."

I huff out a laugh despite the ache in my chest.

"Do you really think this is going to last forever?" She continues, voice gentler now. "The noise? The frenzy? It burns hot and fast, then the world moves on." She shakes her head. "This too shall pass. You and Larkin will become yesterday's news by tomorrow."

She reaches a hand out then and covers one of mine. "But him? The way he looks at you? The way you breathe when he's near?" Her eyes soften. "That's the thing that stays."

I look at my baby. I look at my packed bag on the floor.

The one I never unpacked, because I couldn't admit what leaving felt like.

"I'm scared," I whisper.

"Good." Bri pats my knee. "If it wasn't scary, it wouldn't be worth it."

"I have to go back." I confess, my heart thundering at the realization. "I don't want to lose him, Bri."

"Then don't." She stands, grabbing not only her mug, but mine as well as she starts toward the kitchen. "There's just one thing you need to know though."

I tilt my head, wondering what else there could be. "What's that?

"I'm coming with you."

LATER THAT NIGHT I kiss Larkin's sleeping head and tell her I love her more than the sky and the stars and sound itself. My mom watches from the doorway, no judgement, only under-standing and strength looking back at me.

I'm hoping to leave her with my mom only long enough to see Luc and convince him I want to stay. No matter what. And hope it's not too late. She promises me she'll keep her safe and smother her in snuggles.

"Go," she whispers, brushing my hair like I'm five again. "Find your heart."

BRI and I walk into the venue with pit wristbands. One of the crew, bless his soul, slips us inside before the rest of the crowd can enter, making sure we score dead-center barricade spots in front of the stage.

My heart is trying to exit my body through my throat. Bri hands me the sign we worked on in the hotel room. It's a huge poster board, the red permanent marker still smelling faintly sharp. I clutch onto the rolled sign like a life line. What I wrote will either bring Luc and I back together, or break us apart for good. My fingers shake around the cardboard. "What if he doesn't-"

"Stop." Bri grins. "He will."

"Will it be weird for you to see Dean?" My question a bit hesitant, not sure I should even bring the subject up, but it's eventual that they will see each other. "You know, after hooking up with him."

"God, no!" She laughs out loud, and I think at my obvious embarrassment. "I got exactly what I wanted from that man; an amazing memory. I don't need anything else from him."

"You sure?" I raise a brow. "He's pretty good looking, and nice, most of the time."

"Positive." No hesitation in her response. "It was fun, but it was one and done. That's how he operates."

"Yeah, that's definitely what I've noticed." I murmur, cheeks flaring again, glad we at least have this problem covered.

Time drags as we wait for the arena to fill with people, and then for the opening band to come on. They're not the same band that played in San Francisco and Portland. We're in Seattle, and apparently, they must change up the band based on the city they're in.

Maybe it's a good thing though. Less of a chance for anyone to recognize me and tell Luc I'm here. They finish their set, the lights popping on, the bright light a stark contrast to the darkness we were in just a second ago.

Bri and I both squint at each other, as she reminds me, unnecessarily I might add, what's about to happen. "It's almost time."

"Yep." I bob my head up and down. I'm beyond nervous.

"You look really cute, if that helps." She tosses out, smiling at me. What I'm wearing isn't an accident. I chose it on purpose. To hopefully remind Luc of the night we met. Even though I don't remember it. I know he does.

The lights drop. The crowd roars. My pulse races and I hold my breath as I wait for the band to step on stage. I know their set list. I know which song Luc will open up with. So, I know he'll have a few seconds to look out into the crowd before he sings.

What I don't know, is what he'll do when he does.

Chapter 28
Luc

All I Want
Kodaline

THE LIGHTS HIT, the crowd roars, and the adrenaline kicks like it always does. It's hot, electric, familiar. My pulse syncs to the drums. My lungs expand with that primal rush that tells me I'm home.

But tonight, something feels… off. Like my bones know a truth my head hasn't caught up to yet. The first chord of Dean's riff strums out. I step up to the mic, opening my eyes as I lift my head, and then I see why.

Front and Center. Right in front of me. Right under the lights. It's *her*. My Lily. Her hair loose, eyes wide, breath shaking. She wearing the little red skirt and white tank top she had on the very first night we met. Her arms are raised high, holding a sign like she built it out of hope and terror and every heartbeat we ever shared.

LUC, I LOVE YOU

My world *stops.* The arena noise distorts then muffles like someone shoved my head underwater. My fingers freeze on the mic. My throat closes around the lyrics before they can leave.

For a heartbeat, I think I'm hallucinating. Is this grief? Am I dreaming her existence the way I did every night she was gone? But then she blinks fast, terrified and brave all at once.

And it hits me. She came back. *She came for me.* My chest fractures, pressure and relief slamming together so hard I swear my knees might give.

Dean follows my gaze. He sees her, sees the sign, and lets out a low, "Holy shit."

Sadie doesn't take her eyes off Lily. Arms crossed, sporting a soft smirk like she knew this would happen.

The crowd follows my stare and a ripple goes through them; confusion, then realization, then screaming. Phones rise like a field of lightning.

But all I see is her. My girl. My future. My proof the universe sometimes gives second chances.

I step away from the mic, motioning with my chin for Dean and Hayden to follow me. I stop in front of Mikey's drum kit, then speak to all three of them.

"You mind sitting this first song out?" I twist around to glance toward Lily, who's wearing an expression of pure fear on her face. "I got one I want to sing. Just me."

"Sure." Hayden.

"Go for it." Dean.

"Whatever, mother fucker." Mikey, of course.

I grab a guitar off one of the racks, sling it over my shoulder, and then step back to the mic. I stare down at Lily and point to her, my voice barely stable. "This one. This one is hers. It's called *Anchor In The Noise*."

Silence drops like destiny. I play the first chord. The arena breathes with me. And I sing *her song*.

The one I wrote like a prayer and a confession, the one that hurt to breathe into existence, the one I didn't think she'd ever hear in person. Every lyric I wrote bleeding truth.

I've been chasing thunder,
Living loud enough to drown
Every whisper of the quiet
That I never thought I'd want around.

Crowds screaming like they're saving me,
Lights bright enough to blind
But peace hit me in freckles
And blue eyes that crossed state lines.

And I swore I was fire,
Untouchable, untamed
Till you showed me burning
Doesn't always mean flames.

You were sunlight in a storm,
Warm hands holding all my noise
I was lost in neon chaos,
You were steady, you were choice.

I thought love was just a lyric,
Till you turned it into voice—
When the world gets loud, I find you,

Michelle Windsor

You're my anchor in the noise.

I've been worshiped in the madness,
Been adored and left alone,
Built a kingdom out of stage lights
Never felt like it was home.

But your laugh in the morning,
Little footsteps on the floor
They were louder than my spotlight,
Now I can't run anymore.

Yeah I swore I was chaos,
A wildfire with no end
But you walked through my wreckage
Like you could teach flames to bend.

I thought love was just a lyric,
Till you turned it into voice—
When the world gets loud, I find you,
You're my anchor in the noise.

And if distance was a lesson,
I learned every aching mile
If fear keeps you from choosing us,
I'll wait forever for that smile.

Baby, no halos here,
Just a man who's come undone
But if you'll have me, I will stand,
I don't run from what I won.

You're the calm inside the thunder,
You're the truth I didn't choose
But the heart don't ask permission,
It just beats and prays it won't lose.

And I'll search every shadow,
Every echo of your voice
If it takes forever, I'll find you—
You're my anchor in the noise.

My anchor... in the noise.

I WHISPER THE LAST LINE, eyes locked on her. When the last note fades, her eyes fill. Mine almost do. But I don't break. I'm completely alive in this moment.

I don't even think. I just move. I step to the edge of the stage and hold out my hand. It's not demanding. It's not claiming. It's an invitation. It's a promise.

"Come here, angel." For half a second she just stands there, trembling. Then she nods.

Briana nudges her, and Lily climbs over the barricade into my arms like she belongs nowhere else.

The arena erupts, but I barely hear it. I wrap my hand around her waist and pull her onto the stage, into my chest. Into my life. Into every beat I have left. Mic still in hand, breath unsteady, soul wide open, I rest my forehead against hers.

"You came back," I whisper, voice breaking on the edges.

"No more running." She whispers back. "Not from this, not from us."

I don't care if the world hears. I want them to. I turn to

the crowd, arm around her, heart in my damn throat, and yell into the mic.

"This is Lily. She is my everything. And I'm not hiding her or that ever again. And fuck anyone that has a problem with that!"

The stadium explodes. But I only feel her fingers curling into my shirt, grounding me like she did in a dark bus in the middle of nowhere, her voice in my ear, "I love you."

I kiss her, slow, sure, sacred, and the world goes blindingly, beautifully loud around us.

And for the first time in my life, I don't care who's watching.

She's here. She's mine. And I am hers, every damn note in my body. I thought music was my purpose. Turns out it was the road I was on. That road that led me to them.

Epilogue
Lily

Here Comes The Sun
The Beatles

Six Weeks Later

HOTEL SUITES USED to intimidate me. All that space. All that shine. All that cold perfection.

Now? This one feels like home.

Not because of the velvet sofas or the bay glittering outside the floor-to-ceiling windows, though Boston looks like it's trying very hard to seduce us, but because of the chaos inside it.

Luc's bandmates are sprawled around the giant dining table like it's Thanksgiving and someone spiked all the pies with tequila. Marie is bouncing Larkin on her lap as if she's auditioning for "World's Most Devoted Grandma." Larkin is squealing at a spoon like it's the most magical object ever created. Hayden and Cherry are on the couch, heads bent together as they share something private.

I'm not sure what the hell is going on between Dean and Sadie, but something is. They keep stealing glances at each other. There's too much friction, too much tension. Too much of an attempt at pretending to hate each other when we all know better.

Luc catches my eye from across the table. He doesn't smile big. He does that quiet thing he does, where his mouth softens and his eyes warm and it feels like I'm the only person in the room. I'm doomed. I'm blissfully, willingly doomed.

"I'm telling you," Mikey says, pointing a fork at Marie. "That baby's going to love drumsticks more than guitars. I can feel it."

"Bro, she put mashed carrots in your hair ten minutes ago." Luc deadpans.

"She was blessing me with creativity." Mikey flicks his bangs dramatically, carrot puree and all.

I snort. Loudly. I'm not even embarrassed anymore. Further down the table, Sadie lifts her wine glass without looking at him. "Or marking her territory so no other toddler tries to claim you. Which, honestly, appropriate."

Dean shoots her a sideways glance, seemingly bothered that she just complimented Mikey. Sadie arches a brow, unbothered, sipping her wine like he's background noise. If sexual tension had a sound, it would be the static buzzing between them.

Marie sighs loudly behind us. "We should have more of these family style meals."

Dean mutters, "Only if someone gets Mikey a bib."

Luc leans in, lips brushing my hairline. "You happy?" he murmurs.

I look at Larkin giggling at a crumpled napkin. At my mom smiling like this is the best job she's ever had. At a band that has slowly started to feel like a family I didn't know I'd ever get. At the man whose hand stays on me like he still can't quite believe we found our way back. "More than I thought I could be," I say softly.

Together, we made the decision that Larkin and I will go and live with Luc at his house outside of Chicago afterwards. It's going to be an adjustment, for all of us. But, I figure, if we could live and survive on a bus for over two months, being together in a house should be a piece of cake.

What I've realized in the short time we've been together, is that it doesn't matter where we are. Being with him just feels like home.

He turns my chin and kisses me, slow and sure, ignoring the groans from the peanut gallery.

"Get a room," Mikey tosses a napkin at them.

"Leave them alone," Sadie and Dean say at the same time, Then smile at each other. The rest of us pretend not to notice.

Luc looks at our daughter, then at me. "We good?"

I smile, warm and full. "We're perfect."

He cups my cheek, eyes soft. "Yeah," he agrees in a whisper. "We are."

Larkin squeals again, grabbing at a toy guitar sitting on the table.

"See?" Dean leans forward, grinning. "Guitarist."

Mikey snorts. "Not if she inherits an ounce of taste."

"Hey!" He pouts, acting like he's been shot in the chest.

"You walked into that one." Mikey chuffs, proud of himself.

Luc laughs quietly against my hair as they bicker again. And for the first time in a long time, all the noise feels beautiful.

We are a mess. We are chaos. We are loud and imperfect and stitched together with love and second chances. But we are a family.

And I wouldn't change a single beat.

The End... at least for now.

Devil's Riff, book two in the Devil's Halo Rockstar Series, featuring Dean and Sadie's story, is available for pre-order at https://geni.us/devilsriffebook, and will be releasing March 10, 2026.

Here's a little teaser blurb for you:

Dean Ross doesn't do love songs. Lead guitarist of global rock phenomenon Devil's Halo, he lives by one rule on tour and off: one and done. Heartbreak at seventeen taught him happily-ever-after is a myth, and he's made damn sure to never be the fool twice.
Enter Sadie Brooks, the razor-sharp photojournalist from *Amped Music* assigned to shadow the band for two unfiltered months.
Her job? Capture the soul of Devil's Halo.
Her problem? Dean Ross.

Devil's Muse

He hates her lens. She hates his ego.
The band bus is small. The nights are long.
The chemistry? Combustible.
The more she invades his shadows, the more she becomes
the only sound he can't silence. Desire turns dangerous and
the man who vowed never to fall, might just crash the
hardest.

Devil's Beat, book three in the Devil's Halo Rockstar Series,
featuring Mikey and Quinn's story, is available for
pre-order at https://geni.us/devilsbeatebook,
and will be releasing April 21, 2026.

Devil's Bass, book four in the Devil's Halo Rockstar Series,
featuring Hayden and Vanessa's story is available for
pre-order at https://geni.us/devilsbassebook
and will be releasing June 2, 2026.

Want to stay up to date with all my book news, releases, and
sales?
Sign-up for my weekly newsletter:
https://geni.us/mwindsornewsletter

Devil's Muse Playlist
Available for Download on Spotify

1. Shoot Tequila by Tigirlily Gold
2. Rockstar by Nickelback
3. Sympathy For The Devil by The Rolling Stones
4. How Soon is Now by The Smiths
5. Cover Me In Sunshine by Pink
6. Devil Inside by INXS
7. Bloody Valentine (Acoustic) by Machine Gun Kelly
8. Lovesong by The Cure
9. I Was Made For Lovin' You by YUNGBLUD
10. Time in a Bottle by YUNGBLUD
11. Sparks Fly by Taylor Swift
12. Angels Like You by Miley Cyrus
13. Dead Inside by Blackbear
14. We Are The Champions by Queen
15. The Night We Met by Lord Huron & Pheobe Bridgers
16. All Too Well by Taylor Swift
17. My Only Angel by YUNGBLUD & Aerosmith
18. Change by YUNGBLUD

19. Dad by Michele Morrone
20. Right Now by Van Halen
21. Head's Carolina, Tail's California by Jo Dee Messina
22. The Adventure by Angels & Airways
23. Electric Love by Borns
24. More Than Words by Extreme
25. Breathe by Anna Nalick
26. Play This When I'm Gone by Machine Gun Kelly
27. Everlong (Acoustic Version) by Foo Fighters
28. All I Want by Kodaline
29. Here Comes The Sun by The Beatles

DEVIL'S HALO

New Orleans, LA	May 2	Seattle, WA	June 18
New Orleans, LA	May 3	Seattle, WA	June 19
Dallas, TX	May 7	Salt Lake City, UT	June 21
Dallas, TX	May 8	Salt Lake City, UT	June 22
Dallas, TX	May 9	Lincoln, NE	June 26
Oklahoma City, OK	May 13	Lincoln, NE	June 27
Oklahoma City, OK	May 14	Memphis, TN	July 2
Topeka, KS	May 16	Memphis, TN	July 3
Topeka, KS	May 17	Orlando, FL	July 8
Denver, CO	May 20	Orlando, FL	July 9
Denver, CO	May 21	Atlanta, GA	July 12
Denver, CO	May 22	Atlanta, GA	July 13
Santa Fe, NM	May 25	Raleigh, NC	July 16
Santa Fe, NM	May 26	Raleigh, NC	July 17
Phoenix, AZ	May 29	New York City, NY	July 22
Phoenix, AZ	May 30	New York City, NY	July 23
Phoenix, AZ	May 31	Boston, MA	July 26
Las Vegas, NV	June 3	Boston, MA	July 27
Las Vegas, NV	June 4	Pittsburgh, PA	July 31
Los Angeles, CA	June 6	Pittsburgh, PA	August 1
Los Angeles, CA	June 7	Indianapolis, PA	August 5
San Francisco, CA	June 10	Indianapolis, PA	August 6
San Francisco, CA	June 11	Chicago, IL	August 8
Portland, OR	June 13	Chicago, IL	August 9
Portland, OR	June 14	Chicago, IL	August 10

BURNING IT DOWN

2025 TOUR SCHEDULE

FIFTY SHOWS IN 100 DAYS

Acknowledgments

There are so many people I feel like I need to thank after finishing this story. It's the first full-length book I've written in three years. There was a point where I almost threw in the towel and walked away from writing altogether.

And it wasn't because I didn't like writing. I did. I love it. I have SO many stories knocking around in my head. But there was so much *other* noise that kept me from believing I was good enough, had what it took to be in this business, could write a story and still do ALL the other things that were required of me; social media, marketing, the planning, and oh yeah, being a wife and mom who takes care of our family full-time.

But then, a few years ago, at an annual writing retreat I've been attending for several years, hosted and organized by Lydia Michaels, I found myself surrounded by a group of women who ultimately have become pillars of strength for me. These women, and what they mean to me – words don't seem like enough for me to be able to explain it in a way that would ever truly express my gratitude, my love for them.

These women are fierce, loyal, have brilliant business minds, unlimited kindness, words of encouragement, courage, empathy, extremely generous hearts, unfiltered emotions, strength, and ways of making me laugh that I didn't know were possible. Their unwavering belief that every one of us deserves success and does whatever they can to help each other achieve it is priceless. It's a rarity to find friendships like this, and I don't take a single one for granted. Meredith Wild, DD Lorenzo, Samantha Cole, Ellie Masters, Alexandra Hale, Willow Winters, Amber Vasquez, Vanessa Zion; you ladies have saved me in a way I will never ever be able to repay. Thank you for every second we've spent together, and will continue to spend together.

The woman at the top of this list, the one who has known me the longest, who has listened to me the most, given me more advice, love, friendship, unwavering loyalty, shoving me - sometimes with my feet dragging, toward my goals, is Lydia Michaels. I knew the moment we discovered our mutual love of everything Family Stone, sarcasm, full moons, wine, being sharks -not fucking mermaids (even though I do love sparkles), loving (and sometimes loathing) our husbands, evil clown delight, and being *so fucking perfect*, we would be friends. I just didn't realize how much your friendship would come to mean to me, and how it helped me to become me again. I know you'll get that, even if no one else will. Love you always.

My husband. This man. He is truly my number one fan. He has been cheering me on from the day I wrote my first word, and was still right here beside me today when I finally typed 'the end' to celebrate with me. He is such a man of worth. His happiness comes from mine, and he does everything to make sure I am. He never complains when I'm still in my pajamas at four in the afternoon because I was writing all day, or when I ask if we can order take-out for the third time in a week, or forget to feed the dog and cats because I've lost track of time up in my office. I got one of the good ones. I really did. I probably don't say it enough, but I love you and am so blessed to share this life with you.

A huge shout-out to Lee Ching, my cover designer, for not only this book, but several of my more recent books, and the three Devil books still to come. She is not only extremely talented, but so damn kind and patient. I change my mind like the wind. I'll send her random messages about an idea I have and she always humors me with a polite response, even though I'm sure she's shaking her head most of the time. She brought my vision of my rockstars to life. Thank you for everything Lee.

To my very first readers of this series, and also very close friends, Julie Smith, Natalie Jones, and Amber Vasquez – thank you for always wanting to read my stories, for your feedback, and for your belief in me and my words. I love you ladies.

To Maddison Broughton, whom I definitely think possesses magic in her soul. Speaking of patience, she's got it in spades, and I'm so thankful for that. I get excited about ideas that pop into my orbit, and I ALWAYS want to act on them immediately, and she ALWAYS orders me to take a breath—reminding me, *we have a schedule*!! She keeps me on track, my socials popping, and me sane. She's the best and I'm so grateful to have her on my team.

To the rest of my family; my mom, my sisters, my daughter and two sons, my nieces Grace and Haley, thank you for all your love and support. Thank you for always listening to me ramble to you about the latest story I'm writing and letting me bounce ideas off of you. Thank you for always supporting me, sharing my posts, telling your friends about me, coming to see me. Love you all so much.

Last, but definitely not least, to my readers, whom

without I would be so much less than I am. Whether this is the first story of mine you've read, or the fourteenth, please know how much you mean to me. That you spent your time, which is always a valuable thing, to read my book is something I don't take for granted. I hope this story, or any of my stories, allowed you to escape for a little while, maybe fall in love for a little while, and will live in your heart for a long time. Please know, you all live large in mine.

About the Author

Michelle Windsor is a best selling author of over a dozen contemporary romance stories. She lives in Massachusetts, in a suburb north of Boston, with her husband of over twenty-five years. She's a lover of crystal energy, the phases of the moon, her cats Teddy and Luna, and believes there's not much that can't be solved over a glass or two of prosecco with her beloved sisters.

You can find out more about Michelle, as well as links to all her books, on her webpage: www. authormichellewindsor.com

Stay up to date with all Michelle's news by signing up for her weekly newsletter: https://geni.us/mwindsornewsletter

Also by Michelle Windsor

Michelle's books can be purchased directly in her shop for 20% less than all major retailers, but are available everywhere.

https://shop.authormichellewindsor.com/collections/all

The Auction Series

The Winning Bid

The Final Bid

The Ultimate Bid

The Tempting Nights Series

Tempting Secrets

Tempting Tricks

Tempting Justice

Tempting Teacher

Stand-Alones

Losing Hope

Love Notes

Catching Chase

Landing The Boss

Green Mountain Valley Series

Just One Christmas

Snowflake Wishes and Kisses

Devil's Halo Rockstar Romance Series

Devil's Muse

Devil's Riff

Devil's Beat

Devil's Bass

<u>Omnibus Collections</u>

The Auction Series

Tempting Nights

Seduction in the City